I0566334

Margaret in Manhattan

Also by R. L. Rhyse

Margaret of Greenwich - Margaret and Erika

Margaret at War - Margaret in Tokyo

Margaret and Eve - Margaret and Velda

Margaret and Emily - Margaret and Hillary

Margaret in London - Margaret at Barnard

Margaret at Barnard/Part Two: Deliverance

Margaret in Berlin

R. L. Rhyse

Margaret in Manhattan
Book Thirteen in the
Margaret of Greenwich® Series

Wyston Books, Inc.

Margaret in Manhattan

Wyston Books, Inc.

www.magaretofgreenwich.com

www.wystonbooks.com

R. L. Rhyse

Margaret in Manhattan: a novel

Book Thirteen in the Margaret of Greenwich® Series

1. Margaret of Greenwich (Fictitious character)

2. Teenage Girls Fiction

Library of Congress Control Number: 2017946290

ISBN 978-0-9991057-0-2

eISBN 978-0-9991057-1-9

Cover Photograph by PeopleImages/
Licensed from Getty Images

BISAC: YAF022000 (Girls & Women)
YAF011000 (Coming of Age)
YAF029000 (Law & Crime)

Don't give your enemy half a break.

–Margaret

Margaret in Manhattan

Chapter 1

Coming home implies a joyous reunion but I didn't expect mine to last. Not once my parents learned the shocking news.

After distributing gifts, I said what all wanted to hear: my study in Berlin had gone great and I was looking forward to returning to Barnard College in the fall. But that wouldn't happen. School was already a fading memory, lost in the onrushing inevitable event.

Yet though unplanned pregnancies are common, the question still haunted me: Was my baby's conception accidental?

Hoping to keep the conversation far from babies, I proclaimed that German bread was wonderful and we should order it online. Melanie, my fifteen-year-old sister, chimed in with her culinary experiences. She had been on a school trip to Germany two months earlier.

Then my older sister, Melody, complimented my "more mature" appearance. Did she mean my bigger breasts? I wondered.

Everything was going OK until it suddenly wasn't. I pressed my fist to my mouth and ran to the nearest bathroom to vomit.

After that, the cat was nearly out of the bag, if this isn't too indelicate a phrase to describe being pregnant.

"Probably a touch of the flu," I casually remarked upon returning.

Margaret in Manhattan

My parents had smiled sympathetically but Melody's suspicious look told me that our frank talk was unavoidable.

Chapter 2

Some family's dinners are quiet with little more being said than "pass the butter." Mine were never like that. During our's, personal events were continually shared with content differing by age.

Claudine, the youngest, had just turned eight. Melanie was fifteen, I was nineteen, and Melody was twenty-three. At our meals, the younger children would be advised by their elders though all chimed in.

Since Melody shared her dating disasters only with me, our father's goings-on were the most interesting. He is a respected lawyer in Greenwich with a legal pedigree going back to his great grandfather who had been Chief Justice of the Connecticut Court of Appeals. Though this makes our father sound stuffy, he very definitely is not.

As we ate, I my vegetarian turkey and the others their real meat loaf, my parents began staring at me. Fearing *that* question, I looked frantically toward my sisters, resembling, I thought, an escaping convict.

My father's description of his current legal case saved me. It kept away *the* unwanted question though I knew this relief could only be temporary. Still, like many confronting a disagreeable task, I had hoped to put it off for as long as possible.

Yet even apart from my torment, that dinner's atmosphere had seemed unusually quiet. My parents looked troubled and their conversation was halting unlike their usual chatter. A pall lay over the table. But before my earlier rush to vomit, everything had seemed normal. Or as normal as it ever got with my family.

Were my parents worrying about my health despite my facile lie? Had my father's Lyme disease returned? It had crippled him for years. Was someone else sick? My childhood brush with death, from a heretofore believed fatal genetic illness, had traumatized me to any hint of sickness.

I hesitated to look toward my parents for an answer. Instead, I waited.

My father spoke of his recent case. A local girl, Lydia, had been arrested for shoplifting which is a common teenage crime. Considering it a prank, they don't realize that any arrest is serious and being arrested for a felony will plague their life.

While I didn't know Lydia, her older sister, Jill, had been a masterful shoplifter who was never arrested.

Lydia's parents had hired my father as her lawyer. He hoped to get the felony charge reduced to a misdemeanor and her case transferred from the Criminal Court into the Family Court where her record would be sealed.

"I can't imagine why she did such a dumb thing," my father exclaimed.

"It could be genetic," I said, only half-joking, before telling *my* story.

Chapter 3

"We all thought that Jill was a wizard," I began.

Everyone at the table stopped eating, recognizing that mine would be *some* story.

"Each day she came to school in a new expensive outfit. Her father managed a fishing tackle store and wasn't well-off so we wondered. The cost of her outfits ran into the hundreds of dollars.

"These changed regularly until suddenly they didn't. She was back to wearing the same cheap jeans and shirts that I wore. Nosiness got the better of me and I asked her.

"'I shoplifted, of course,'" she explained.

"Why did you stop? Were you arrested?" I asked.

"'No, never,'" Jill replied.

"Well?" I persisted.

"Jill looked around the hallway before answering. Other kids passed us but they were into their heads and we were alone. 'Walk with me and I'll tell you,' she said, and I did.

"'Two weeks ago, I was walking through the Mall. My shopping bags were filled with clothes that I'd stolen. It had been a good day and I felt pleased, a little nervous but satisfied too.

"'While leaving the Mall, I thought of calling my boyfriend, Erik. Just before reaching the exit, a guard ran in front of me. When he turned and faced the departing customers, I almost died on the spot.

"'I love CSI and want to be an FBI profiler but saw that plan going up in flames. Then, thinking quickly and turning from him, I opened the top two buttons of my shirt. Erik likes me braless and when I turned back I was hanging out.

"'At the door, I gave the guard my biggest smile and he didn't look further than my breasts. 'Good afternoon, miss,' he said, holding the door for me. I nearly collapsed when I reached my car. That was when I stopped shoplifting.'"

Chapter 4

The room lay silent when I finished my story. No one seemed to know what to say so I looked toward my father and spoke.

"Lydia's family doesn't have money. Can they afford to hire you?" I asked.

"I accepted their case pro bono, as my contribution to the town where we've lived for so long. People helped us when we were down and it's the right thing to do," he replied.

My father couldn't work during the years that Lyme disease disabled him. Our family survived with aid from Social Security Disability payments and food from the Mormon Food Bank and local farmers who were past clients of my father.

"Who can tell what Lydia will become if given help. How many people do you know who haven't made a mistake in their life?" my mother asked, solemnly.

None of us risked an answer and she bowed her head.

"Let us pray," she said.

Her four daughters lowered their heads and prayed, without the trace of a smile.

My prayer seemed answered when my youngest sister raised *her* worry. I've dodged the bullet for now, I thought.

"There's this boy, Ryan, who wants to hang out with me. We play the same video game," Claudine said, hesitantly.

Our mother looked up sharply. She smelled the hint of impropriety though I didn't.

"What's wrong with that?" I asked, though feeling that the phrase "hang out with me" was a bit early to use for a boy and a girl of their age. Her hanging out with a girl I would have understood. Still, times change, I told myself.

"Well, he's nice to me, holding the door and offering me snacks. But he's always getting into trouble. He just got detention for a joke."

"What did he do?" Melanie asked.

"He put a rubber spider on a girl's pizza and she freaked out," Claudine replied.

"That's not nice," I said calmly, and Claudine nodded agreement.

"He might be doing these things to show that he's unhappy, as a cry for help. What are his parents like?" my mother asked.

"I don't know but he called his stepmother a ..."

Claudine hesitated to say the word but we understood.

"It's good that you're worried. People are judged by their company and you might be encouraged to go down the wrong path. Still, why not invite him and his parents for lunch on Saturday? You two could hang out while we get to know them and see if we can help," my mother said.

"That's a *great* idea," I seconded.

Claudine beamed. Her problem was solved.

I turned toward my mother.

"You really are an angel," I said, and meant it.

But my mother's sad eyes told me that my compliment hadn't registered and my father turned toward me.

"We have to speak with you after dinner," he said, gravely.

His tone was what he used when speaking of a client who had lost their critical case.

Chapter 5

After dinner was a half-hour later in my father's home-office. Instead of sitting in his favored La-Z-Boy recliner, my father sat with my mother on the sofa and I sat in a club chair facing them. Anxiety washed over me as I noted their grim faces.

"What is it?" I asked hurriedly, being unable to bear their silence.

It had usually been my father who began serious talks but then my mother spoke first.

"Have you spoken with Lena recently?" she asked, hesitantly.

Lena is her sister and my biological mother. My adoptive mother had resented her sister for years, needlessly fearing that she would wean my affection from my adoptive family. They had reconciled only months earlier.

"No, I didn't, things being so rushed. Is something wrong?"

"She wants to see you. Go this evening. She's at home," my father said.

His tone was calm but tears welled in my mother's eyes as he spoke.

"I'll go now," I said, getting up.

"Take the Camaro," my father said.

He rose and tossed me the car keys. My mother hugged me tightly before I left. It was as if she feared that I might not return.

Margaret in Manhattan

Lena lived in a condominium just off Greenwich Avenue. Though only in her early forties, she had been widowed from two happy marriages. Having done "the estate thing," as she put it, she was content to live in a worry-free apartment, possibly because she was rarely there.

Lena worked long hours managing the local psychiatric hospital that she owned and consulting across America. Because of her busy schedule, most of our meetings had been in her office. Going to her apartment was unusual though I was always welcome there.

Lena buzzed me into the complex and I rode the elevator with muddled worries. Was she ill? Was she moving from the area? I would soon find out.

When she opened the door, my initial emotion was shock. I had never seen her without makeup and dressed so carelessly. Her pajamas were creased and her robe was stained. I hope that it's not blood, I prayed. Please, God, let it not be blood!

Chapter 6

We hugged, and I spoke first.

"I should have spoken with you before going to Berlin but things just happened," I said, apologetically.

"Things happen," Lena said, simply, hugging me and leading me to the kitchen.

"Are you hungry?" she asked, the typical question of mothers.

"No, I just ate."

She reached for the coffee pot and poured herself a cup. Being a lapsed Mormon, she no longer followed the religion's prohibition against drinking coffee but this didn't bother me. So long as others don't infringe on my freedom, I'm willing to extend it to them.

"I wanted to speak with you," Lena said.

I waited, being unable to stop glancing at the stain on her robe.

"I went through a bit of a crisis while you were away," she said.

"A crisis," I repeated.

"Just so."

There was more silence. Lena poured a bit more cream into her coffee, then stirred it with the spoon even more slowly. She was having a hard time getting started.

"Are you OK?" I asked, finally, in what I intended was the non-nonsense tone of my lawyer-father.

"I think so. Can anyone be sure?" Lena replied.

No, she isn't OK, I told myself. Lena managed a hospital, was an award-winning lecturer, and had been a guest at the White House. The uncertain woman standing before me wasn't the Lena that I knew. Something big must have happened to her while I was away, I decided, and asked.

"What *happened*?"

Lena sipped her coffee before answering. When she did, it was with a question.

"Have you ever heard of subcutaneous panniculitis-like T-cell lymphoma, SPTCL?"

Some statements are so shocking that it takes a moment to understand what was said. Lena's question was like the rumbling of an earthquake.

Guilt coursed through me after she spoke. I should have been with her and not in Berlin. I couldn't bear losing her. Not after learning that she was *not* my aunt, as I had been told since childhood, but was my biological mother.

Love comes in different shapes and sizes and ours had come late.

Chapter 7

My interest has always been more literature than science but even I knew that lymphoma is a type of cancer and not good news.

"No, I've never heard of it," I replied.

"That's not surprising since it's rare," Lena said.

"*OK*," I said slowly, now regaining control of myself despite the tears.

"It's a story," Lena said.

"I'm listening. I'll take a juice now," I said.

I wasn't thirsty but sensed that doing something ordinary would calm her. I could see that she was as nervous as me. One day, inevitably, the child becomes as the mother though I hadn't expected this to happen so soon.

Lena was calmer when she returned. I took my time opening the juice box. Though having the purple color of wine, it is simply juice, I told myself, and thus isn't forbidden to Mormons. This weird thought evidenced how crazy my thinking became since I left home that evening.

I'm not usually a worrier but medical issues can terrify me. Without meaning to, Lena was doing a good job of this. I learned forward to indicate that I was listening closely.

"A month ago, I found a small lump on my body. It didn't hurt but was just there. I made an appointment with my internist who sent me to a surgeon. The lump was removed and the surgeon said that he would call me with the result of the biopsy as soon as he got it.

"I phoned his office a week later when he hadn't called. They said that they hadn't yet received the results. The surgeon called three days later and said that he wanted to see me that afternoon. 'You have subcutaneous panniculitis-like T-cell lymphoma, SPTCL. It's a rare cancer,' he said.

"The lab results had taken so long because the condition is so infrequent that the opinion of a second lab was sought. They confirmed the original finding and he scheduled an appointment with an oncologist for me.

"I Googled SPTCL after leaving his office. What I learned is that it is a terminal, fast-acting disease. Even with the most recently discovered treatment, no one with SPTCL has lived longer than two years."

I stopped sipping the juice, no longer being able to swallow. More tears flowed down my cheeks. Lena left her chair and led us to the living room. There, we sat together and hugged. Purple juice dripped onto the costly sofa but such things no longer mattered.

What Lena had told me was shocking but her next information was a bombshell.

"No one knows what I am about to tell you. Two years ago, when I told you of your adoption by my sister, I left out something. I couldn't tell you then because I felt too guilty," Lena said.

I waited. This event seemed even harder for Lena to reveal than her death sentence. Finally, she spoke.

"You have a twin brother. I don't know who adopted him but you must find him for me. Before I die, just as I did with you, he must learn why I placed him for adoption and know that I loved him."

Chapter 8

Years later, it still seemed like there was a *before* and an *after* in my life. *Before*, was my arrival from Berlin, pregnant and happy but uneasy too. *After*, was the meeting with my mother when she told me she was dying, and that I had a twin brother.

Minutes later, I stood paralyzed in the building's lobby, unsure where to go, I told myself that things would never be the same and they never were.

I agreed to my mother's request. No child could have refused. I would find my brother wherever he is, to be assured of his mother's love before we mourned at her grave.

A couple with young children entered the lobby. The woman smiled as she passed me but I didn't respond. I couldn't and wondered if I would ever smile again.

Then, without conscious awareness, I returned to the elevator, pressed "5" and waited. As the door closed and the cage rose, I grew calm, having realized what I most needed at that moment.

As I had expected, it was her son who opened the door. Though vibrantly healthy, Mother Marie was in her eighties and he valued their remaining years together. His wife understood.

It had been months since I last spoke the ancient Yoruba language but the words came readily to me: "Mo fe bo. Ojo o buru, ebo nii gbe ni o." ("I want to worship. In days of turbulence, it is ebo that saves." (*Ebo* is the making of animal or plant sacrifice to one's ancestors or to a deity, *Orisha,* of the Santeria religion.)

Margaret in Manhattan

The man bowed gravely and spoke reverently: "Ka maa worisha. Işe Olorun tobi. Aye l'oja orun n'ile." ("Let us keep looking to the Orisha. God's work is great and mighty. The world is a marketplace. The spirit world is home.")

Though a practicing Mormon, I had adopted the Santeria religion after being healed of a deadly disorder by following Mother Marie's dietary advice. A retired teacher, she had been tutoring me while I was on home instruction, having been too ill to attend school.

Mother Marie is a *babalawo*, a high priest of the Santeria religion and one of the few women permitted to function in that role.

Entering her apartment, I suddenly understood why I had come: to learn my fate and that of my brother and of our mother. *The spirit world is home*, and I had come home.

Chapter 9

Mother Marie didn't have to ask me how I felt. I looked bad! She led me to the living room and asked if I wanted something to drink. I asked for water. When she left the room to get it, I considered what to tell her. *Everything*, I decided, even more than one ordinarily tells a doctor. Her task would be to predict my future and that of my mother and of brother using the ancient African method of Sixteen-Cowrie-Divination.

When Mother Marie returned, she placed the glass of water on the table and waited for me to tell her why I came. Followers of Santeria sought her advice only on urgent matters. I wasted no time drinking and began speaking immediately.

I told her of the career in security that I had chosen and why. I told her of being pregnant, of my mother's dire diagnosis, and of her plea that I find my brother so they might re-unite before her death. I added that, though being twins, we might have different fathers since my mother had been involved with two men at the time of our conception.

I said that I no idea how to proceed and feared that dredging up the past would harm my brother. Then I spoke an ancient proverb in the Yoruba language, "Ohun gbogbo ti a ba se laye la ookule re lorun." ("That which we do on earth, we shall account for kneeling in heaven.")

After speaking, I felt at peace since my fate was now in the hands of the Gods. This may sound strange, my being a Mormon, but, as Mother Marie had once told me, "The Gods are not jealous."

Margaret in Manhattan

The Santeria faith was born in Nigeria which is the origin of the Yoruba people. Many were captured by slave traders and brought to the Americas. Here, their religion spread, hidden by combining it with conventional Roman Catholic rituals. In Cuba, it is known as Lucumi and in Brazil as Macumba.

There are famous Santeria followers in the United States though, from fear of persecution, their worship is not publicized. One of these was Desi Arnez of the past, widely popular *I Love Lucy* show which can still be seen on cable TV.

During the *Diloggún* (divination ceremony), sixteen cowrie shells are used to determine which *pataki* (sacred story) should be studied. Some of these advise a change in behavior or for something to be avoided to elude misfortune. Though ancient, each story is alive in the universe, awaiting connection with our human energies.

Each shell has a natural "mouth" and a value of one. The more shells that fall mouth up, the rarer and stronger is the spiritual current for the foretold events.

As prescribed, I first sprinkled water on the cowrie shells and then prayed to Elegguá, one of the most important gods. He wields great power and knows the past, present, and future.

"Elegguá protect my family.

Grant me long life and peace.

Grant me elevation of my consciousness.

Grant me the ability to use my own hands.

Elegguá I salute you."

The ceremony began.

Chapter 10

By tradition, a cowrie shell is a Nigerian kola nut which has been split into four quarters showing two "male" and two "female" sides. Priests interpret the quarters depending on how they fall when cast.

In the Americas, the foretelling is conducted with four pieces of a coconut shell having a cowrie attached to each side. Two males (shells showing the bulb side) and two females (shells showing the ridges) are cast, and interpretations are made.

There are various depths of prophecy. Mother Marie performed the *Merindilogun* or *Sixteen Cowries*. At this level of inquiry, all spiritual planes become actual with the forces of heaven and earth being unfolded.

During the prayer, Mother Marie first rubbed the shells between her hands. She then placed them in a sacred bowl and I exhaled on them three times. She then touched my forehead with the shells enclosed in her hands and cast them, saying, "Difa fun, Margaret" ("Grant cosmic intelligence to Margaret").

Mother Marie made the prescribed two casts of the shells. The first cast is dominant and the second cast provides a balancing factor. Both were identical: *Ofún: Ten Mouths On The Mat*.

Such an event is rare. A person having this luck could retire after a day's casino gambling. Mother Marie's expression was grave when she spoke.

"There cannot be death without life nor life without death," she said.

Then, as is the religion's tradition, she counseled me by telling me *patakis* (sacred stories). Her first was the ancient tale of how Life and Death walked together in the thin, veiled chasm between Heaven and Earth, where everyone crosses but only they live.

Though side-by-side, each looked in opposite directions. They walked in silence until Death turned to Life and spoke: "One day you will die and your death will make *me* stronger." Life smiled, and said, "One day you will live and your life will make *me* stronger."

Both argued: Death insisted that Life is weak because everything dies, and Life insisted that Death is weak because Life always finds a way to continue. They finally agreed that for this world to exist, both Life and Death were needed for there could be no life without death and no death without life. Having reached this conclusion, they stood together as brothers.

I felt my face turn pale. Had Mother Marie foretold my death or that of my mother or of my brother?

Chapter 11

Noting my pallor, Mother Marie touched my shoulder with a comforting gesture before continuing.

"All must age, including Ochanlá who was once young and vibrant. Weakness brought her fragility and even in Heaven she suffered. Feeling desperate, she went to the heavenly diviner, Ofún.

"'Will I have no more enjoyment despite having followed the will of Olódumare (the supreme deity of the Yoruba) all my life? Now, even in Heaven, I age and am too old to walk without exhaustion.

"'Let us divine and see what the will of Olódumare is for your old age,' the seer said. After conducting the sacred casting ritual, he spoke, 'No, Ochanlá, this isn't your end and you need suffer no longer. Once you make ebó (an offering made to a Yoruba God), matters will become clear.'

"Ochanlá had faith and made ebó, having seen miracles happen to others when they did so on Earth. Then she went to sleep.

"When she awoke, her skin was still wrinkled and her joints were still swollen. But she felt strength and youthfulness as she rose. When she went outside, power coursed through her body. Standing no longer tired her nor did she walk hunched over.

"She felt the sun's caressing rays as she floated from Heaven to Earth. Her previously yellowed garments were now brilliantly white and the sun paid tribute to her with the dazzling new day.

"Thereafter, thanks to the power of Ofún, she was worshipped forever on Earth after her casting result of *Ten Mouths On The Mat*. We must give offering and pray."

We did, and Mother Marie began: "Mo fe bo. Abo ru, Abo ye, Abo şişe." ("I want to worship. May the offerings be carried. May the offerings be accepted. May the offerings bring about change.")

Before leaving Mother Marie's apartment, Heaven's response had vibrated within me: "B'ao ku ishe o tan. Ego fin, Eru da. Dide dide lalafia." ("When there is life, there is still hope. The offerings are accepted, evil forces depart. Arise, arise in peace.")

Chapter 12

What I most needed after leaving Mother Marie was the ear of a good friend. One who would understand without feeling the need to express trite feelings or advice. For this, for me, there was no one better than Erika.

Erika has experienced more than her share of suffering: the murder of her mother and sister; the need to negotiate her father's poor choice of girlfriends; the recent discovery that her fiancée, Clarence, has diabetes. She listens without judging.

Erika's father is a billionaire. Their home's sturdily gated entrance and security rival that of the White House.

I arrived at a little before ten, after gaining a compliment from a guard that I had long known and who was old enough to be my father. I returned his tribute with a forced smile.

Erika was now fully recovered from mononucleosis ("the kissing disease"). She had suffered from this when we last met months before. She was surprised but not alarmed when I arrived so late. We had considered each other as sisters and her house had been my second home for years.

"Am I glad to see *you*," she burst out, as we hugged.

"No more than me," I replied, breaking down in tears.

I told her of Lena's deadly illness, of her plea that I find my twin brother, and of Mother Marie's uncertain prophecy.

"But its ending was favorable: 'When there is life, there is still hope,'" Erika said.

Margaret in Manhattan

Having regained self-control, I agreed, dried my eyes, and looked about the room. By way of relaxing, Erika changes her bedroom's décor every few months. When this began, her father had objected to its cost. "It's cheaper than using drugs," she replied, and he never raised the issue again.

"How can I help?" Erika asked.

I shook my head, still feeling muddled.

"The first thing that you must do is to prioritize," Erika said, firmly.

I slowly nodded agreement.

Erika's eventual goal is to manage her father's business empire. She had sat in on his business meetings for years, being tutored as I was being taught Vladimir's security business. She was *the* planner of high school events. Instinctively organizing relaxes her and she does it well. But she is also tactful and her question revealed this.

"What do you consider should be your priority?" she asked, placing this decision on my shoulders where it belonged.

Chapter 13

Without conscious thought, I seemed to have been making plans since leaving Mother Marie since my answer came quickly.

"The first thing is to tell my parents about Lena's condition. Then, to find my brother. I can't be sure how much time we have until..." I said, stifling a sob.

Erika let the ensuing silence fill the room.

"What can I do?" she asked, finally.

"I don't know. Just be here for me, I guess."

"I always will be."

My eyes glistened with tears.

"I know."

After pulling myself together, I focused on the major task at hand.

"I need to see the records of the agency that placed my brother to find the couple that adopted him," I said.

"They'd never permit that," Erika said.

"I don't plan to ask," I said.

Erika simply nodded. She knew me well enough to know what I was thinking.

"I'll need an introduction to their office, to discover where their records are stored and how secure their storage is. I can't go in and ask. I need a good reason and motive for them to answer. You could help with that," I said.

"How?"

"A letter from your father's charitable foundation stating that it heard of their good work and was considering providing financial support. But before doing so, it would like for several of their staff to learn about their operations and be assured that the funds would be put to good use. Any agency would jump through hoops with that incentive," I said.

"Who would be going?" Erika asked.

"Why we and Randy, of course," I said, with my first real grin that day.

"You're the better writer so get busy. I'll tell my dad's secretary to refer any contact from the agency to me. I've used his name in the past and she's good about such things."

I began writing.

Chapter 14

Writing the letter went quickly. I made it brief since the promise of money doesn't take much persuading. Erika could have written it though I am the better writer.

But her abilities are exceptional. Erika has a vivid imagination and inexhaustible energy. She has a powerful ability to concentrate and a talent for organizing and stimulating others. She has a natural gift for business and, important for our task, a flair for salesmanship. "She'll be a better manager than me," her father had proudly proclaimed.

Sadly, Erika's managerial tasks began when she was young, after the rape and murder of her mother and sister. Though grieving, she had supported her father by helping to run his household, as she would one day help to manage his business empire.

Our letter was mailed on the following day and we received a reply three days later. Signed by the adoption agency's Executive Director, we were invited to discuss our "generous donation" over dinner at the Park Avenue apartment of one of their board members.

The invitation wasn't exactly what I wanted but it would be a start. Afterward, Randy would gain access to their computerized records–I hoped.

"Planning and attitude are the most important elements when engineering a fraud," Erika said.

I looked up from my iPad. I had been reading about the adoption agency online.

"Where did you hear that?" I asked, surprised by her statement.

"I didn't. It's just sensible," she replied.

She was right though I hadn't expected for her to have an interest in fraud.

"How do you know?" I asked.

"Crooks pollute the business world and a good appearance means nothing. Just before the 1929 Wall Street crash, at a bank in Flint, Michigan, fifteen employees sat around a table and created the largest bank fraud that the world had known. At these meetings, thefts of money were programmed for investment into the booming stock market.

"They were skillful thieves but lousy investors. There was no Federal bank insurance then and when the bank collapsed, the lives of many depositors were shattered."

"And fraud will never happen to your father?" I asked.

"Damn straight that it won't!" she replied, hotly.

Our conversation turned to basics: what we would wear to the Agency's dinner, and what we must gain from it.

Chapter 15

Erika is an expert on clothes and takes shopping seriously. For me, throughout the years when my family was poor, our outfits came from the Salvation Army store in nearby Portchester, New York. At that time, second-hand shirts and jeans were my style.

But with her unswerving generosity, Erika often lent and even gifted me whatever clothes I needed, or she felt that I did.

At this dinner, Erika would be the star and dress accordingly. I would be her drab assistant, like the fabled small-town librarian.

"Dress length to your ankles?" Erika asked, with a grin.

"Whatever Madam considers best," I replied, submissively.

"What name should I use?" I asked.

"Margaret is OK. I won't offer your last name during the introduction," Erika said.

Despite her humorous tone, my hurt expression showed.

"I was joking. What is it?" Erika asked, apologetically.

"What you said reminded me of my put-towns from the snooty Manhattan mothers that I babysat for," I said.

"Those days are gone," she said, sympathetically,

Though this was true, the effect of poverty remained. I no longer needed to work as a babysitter since prosperity had returned to my adoptive family.

My biological mother would have given me money but I had never asked, fearing its effect on my sisters, that I could buy what they could not. Adoption or not, we were *one* family.

I hadn't yet told Erika all that happened in Berlin. Not everything is shared, even between sisters. I didn't want to burden her with knowledge of a crime: that I had embezzled, using Randy's computer expertise, twenty-one million dollars. It was the fruit of a notorious criminal's enterprises and I gave some of this money to one of his victims. The rest lay in numbered bank accounts, accessible only by me. I had been Vladimir's apt pupil.

The next morning, Erika and I shopped for suitable clothes at Richards, a Greenwich store known for its service and styles. This trip wasn't needed since we could have worn what we already owned but shopping relaxes Erika.

Erika bought a black, geometric, long-sleeve dress by Alexander McQueen. It had a ribbed mock neckline, nipped in waist, and flared hem. Costing a mere two-thousand-dollars, it was fit for this frugal billionaire's daughter.

To this, Erika added a Ralph Lauren black cardigan and black suede, crystal-beaded, pointed flats by Christian Loubout.

Her entire outfit cost forty-five-hundred dollars and I didn't blink, being used to her shopping ways.

"Now for you," Erika said.

"Dowdy, madam?"

"Definitely, but maybe someday…"

We both grinned.

Chapter 16

I dodged the talk with Melody that day. When I arrived home, she was out on a date and I went immediately to bed. When I arose the next morning, she still hadn't returned.

At twenty-three, Melody was beyond the age when she felt the need to provide an excuse for her behavior. And our parents, despite being religious Mormons, didn't hassle their kids. They trusted them to do the right thing. For me, after learning of my risky involvements in London and Tokyo, they had simply prayed that I would remain safe.

I expected to hear about Melody's date when she returned home from work. That would be when she would grill me too.

I had business to do before then, having decided that I needed help. I had little knowledge of computer security and needed an expert, which Randy was. I hadn't yet told him of my plan though Erika had already informed the agency that there would be *three* guests for dinner. It was time for Randy to learn that he was coming.

Thankfully, Randy doesn't seriously object to my behaving like this. Like most geniuses, he needs someone to deal with the practical aspects of living. Also, because he tends toward being a loner, he relies on me to schedule our social life.

This dinner would be a social event with an agenda: Randy must gain entrée into the Agency's computer system to hack it to get the information that I needed.

Would Randy do this? I doubted that he would refuse my request. First, because he loved me and what I sought was important to me. Also, because the only thing that he loved more than me (until our baby was born!) was a hacking challenge.

"It's a piece of cake," he had said, upon agreeing to my past plea that he hack a computer. I hoped that he would feel the same now.

Chapter 17

First things first, I told myself, as I drove to Randy's house. His parents were now friendly to me after the family blow-up months before. That was when Randy told them that he was accompanying me to Berlin *despite* their objection. To Randy's credit, he had threatened to leave his family, drop out of college, and accept the six-figure job that he had been offered in Austin.

After his wife's quiet persuasion, Randy's father had relented. Thereafter, things went well between us. Or as good as they could considering my future father-in-law's bossy personality. Randy's father isn't bad. He simply has the inflexible character of surgeons who consider themselves God's equal.

After courteously hugging his parents, I sketchily described our life in Berlin, leaving out the illegal events of course. I also left out Randy's long talks with my uncle, Borya. He is a Russian general who is nicknamed *Lucifer*. None of my relatives has been willing to tell me why.

Randy bounded downstairs, gave me a quick kiss, and we went outside. While seated on the tree swing, I told him why I came.

"What I say will come as a shock," I began.

He touched my belly.

"More than *that*?" he asked, playfully with a smile.

"*Please*, they're probably watching," I cautioned.

"*You didn't tell them*?" Randy asked.

"I haven't told my parents yet," I replied.

My serious tone caught his attention and I told him everything: about Lena's lethal illness; the surprising news that I had a twin brother; and my pledge to bring him to her, even if only briefly.

My request didn't take persuading. Randy took my hand, looked me in the eyes and asked, "How can I help?"

Then, despite his parents', we kissed, and I told him what I needed. Randy's response was immediate.

"A piece of cake," he said, assuredly.

Chapter 18

Gaining Randy's agreement to hack was easy but getting him to wear the proper clothing wasn't. Like most techies, Randy dresses in styles popularized by the founders of Google and Facebook.

"They go to *job* interviews in T-shirt, jeans, and sneakers," he insisted.

"*You're* not on a job interview. You'll be pretending to work for a hedge fund and are attending a business dinner in a Park Avenue apartment. These people wear suits, as you well know," I said, feeling annoyed.

My plan is falling apart before it starts, I thought.

"I don't even *own* a suit!" Randy moaned, though I knew that he did.

"That's no problem. We'll buy you one," I said, ending the conversation with my lawyer-dad's no-nonsense look.

That's what we did. Because Erika's father hates shopping, she buys his clothes for him and has become expert with men's fashion too. Thus, she accompanied us to Richard's and made the final selection. Even Randy liked it.

Erika summarized the dress advice that she had gained from her father.

"Your clothes are the first thing to be judged by those who see you so their choice matters a lot. The people that you are meeting should remember you and not your clothes. They must not detract. What you wear should *support* your performance but not *be* a performance. If they feel too old for you, play at being an adult until your inside catches up with how you look," she said.

Erika advised against buying Randy a suit, stating that her father's technical staff never wears them. Instead, she chose a charcoal herringbone cashmere sportscoat by Canali. It had notched lapels and lower front patch pockets. She added a charcoal grey flannel sport shirt, and desert grained leather Chukka boots, Italian shoes by Bontoni.

"These could have been made for him and the prices are *a steal*," the sales clerk said, reassuringly.

Hmm...a bit over four-thousand-dollars is a steal? I asked myself, while paying with a credit card tied to one of my numbered bank accounts. But the clothes were worth it for Randy loved his new outfit. And it would improve his performance when he went "onstage."

Having completed costuming, our preparation continued for the upcoming drama: writing the lines for Erika, Randy, and me.

Chapter 19

Since we didn't know who would be at the dinner, my suggestions were inevitably sketchy.

"Erika should tell about her father's philanthropic activities and how he became interested in adoption. Using my adoption as an example would be safe territory.

"At some point, she'll speak of her father's commitment to data security. That's when Randy, *one of his computer experts,* will ask questions to get the information that he needs to penetrate their system."

I turned toward Randy.

"You had better prepare your lines in advance," I told him.

"A piece of cake," he said.

Everyone has their pet phrase. Randy's had apparently become that. Mine was calling him, "my darling," a line that I had picked up from some old movie years before.

I turned toward Erika. There was one more matter to cover.

"Your father needn't donate money. At some point, you can write to the Agency, stating that his other obligations prevent his involvement and that he doesn't contribute to organizations where he doesn't play an active role," I said.

"We'll see. If I like what I hear, he may contribute. Being on the boards of non-profit organizations is a good way to meet those who count," Erika replied.

You mean, *meeting those who have money and influence*, I thought.

Abram, Erika's bodyguard, drove us to the dinner. Our hostess had been informed that he would attend and they understood. Being obsessed with personal security is how today's super-wealthy live.

The apartment was an eleven-room penthouse duplex, twenty blocks north of Grand Central Terminal. Before the dinner, we had been proudly shown the apartment. From the furnishings, it was obvious that the decorator knew what good design was and what it could do.

Erika's home cost forty-million-dollars. It had been featured in news articles so our tour might have reflected a touch of one-upmanship. Though the apartment lacked Erika's private harbor and tennis court, it *was* impressive.

The kitchen was past conventional showy appliances and fixtures. These were sleek and hidden away, not being visually disruptive. There was a made-to-order mahogany wood island and a gold marble countertop. The hardware and hinges were exceptional.

The living room had a marble-encased gas fireplace and a double-height, twenty-three-foot ceiling that drew attention to the skylight above. A staircase led to a terrace containing a small kitchen and an outdoor shower and cabana. At the end of the walkaround, our expressions of admiration weren't phony.

Chapter 20

It wasn't the small dinner party that we had expected. The sixteen guests included the couple's four-year-old daughter and five-year-old son. Their behavior was amazingly polite for young children.

Next on the agenda, after the introductions and tour, was dinner. Thankfully, this was buffet style. It's embarrassing to be the only vegetarian at a meat-lovers banquet.

I chose the whitefish, baked salmon, and salad. Randy, sitting beside me, had chosen similarly after a glance in my direction. The Russian food that he had gorged on in Berlin had added pounds on him. Despite his good health, I examined what he ate carefully. He was the father of my expectant baby.

Immediately after dinner, the children were sent to bed and we got down to business.

Lindsay, the Chairperson of the Agency's Board, began her spiel. She had apparently been chosen as the primary spokesperson that evening.

"We've been finding loving, adoptive parents for over one-hundred-years. Not only do we arrange adoptions, but we also guide families by providing them with support through our Family Center. It offers therapy for children throughout New York City. How did your father become interested in supporting us?" she asked, with a gleaming smile.

In reply, Erika gave our pitch.

"You can thank *Margaret*," she said, turning toward me with a smile. "We've long been like sisters and she is an adoptee. My father became interested in adoption after recently learning this. He had Randy, his security expert, check on agencies and found that your's had a superb reputation."

Smiles spread across the room as eyes turned toward me. There had been no story for me to learn since I had often told it.

"I was adopted at birth by a Greenwich couple. I recently discovered the identity of my biological parents and the four of us are now close. I spent the past several months with my natural father in Berlin," I said.

"Is he American?" came the logical question.

"No. Vladimir is a former Russian general who now manages a private security company. Abram, Erika's bodyguard, is one of his employees. His partners are former officials of the CIA and the SIS, Britain's Secret Intelligence Service."

I intentionally add these details. Learning that my father had been a Russian General has a chilling effect on conversations.

"How fascinating. Was it an agency adoption?" Lindsay asked, with honest emotion.

"No, the adoptive couple were relatives. My biological mother had been going through a rough period and didn't feel that she could care for me."

I might have made my story more dramatic by adding that no one was sure who my biological father was since my biological mother had been having affairs with two men simultaneously and a DNA test was never performed. But telling that would have been overkill. Though this group was "modern," we were playing it straight.

Erika smoothly turned the conversation back to *our* business.

"With the increase in hacking, my father is greatly concerned with the security of business records and your's among the most sensitive. That's why he asked Randy to accompany us. Don't been fooled by his youth: he's a genius when it comes to computers."

Randy blushed, as he usually does after being given a compliment. Then he gave his patter, seeking an invitation to their office to invade their most sensitive records.

Chapter 21

Erika had earlier advised Randy how to begin his talk.

"First, demonstrate your expertise. Then they'll beg you to check their system for bugs," she said.

And that's what Randy did. He is a born teacher, having the ability to make the most complex technical matter understandable. My fear, before we had used his expertise to embezzle millions, was that he might wind up becoming a teacher. This would force us to live on their low salary and for me to have to continually soothe his hurt feelings. Every school is a massive bureaucracy and Randy couldn't tolerate their idiocy.

"Forty years ago, a revolutionary paper was written. It was called, *New Directions in Cryptography,* and changed how Internet secrets are kept. Earlier, cryptography was a simple matter. You had a key that made unreadable what you had written without it, maybe replacing one letter with another as had been done for a thousand years," Randy began.

"But for the cipher to work, the key had to be kept secret. During World War Two, the allies had *SIGSALY*, a system that scrambled voice communications in real time. The encrypted signal was then sent to another SIGSALY station where it was decrypted. Each message was encoded with a different key, making decrypting much harder."

Though this group wasn't technical, they hung on Randy's every word. He loves to teach and his enthusiasm is contagious.

"The German military used the famed *Enigma* machine for text communication. You can see one at the

National Security Agency's Cryptology Museum in Laurel, Maryland. It consists of a keyboard, wires, a plugboard like a telephone switchboard, rotating wheels, and an output board.

"When a key is pressed, the machine runs through its program design and spits out a different letter which lights up on the board. An identically arranged Enigma machine performs the same actions but in reverse. The key to Enigma's success was that the cypher changed each time that the letter was pressed. Press B and the machine would display R, but when you pressed B again, the machine would show a different letter.

"Both the Enigma and SIGSALY systems were the early equivalent of algorithms that repeatedly conduct a mathematical function. Breaking their code meant learning their underlying procedure, their *key*. But modern cryptology is different.

"Hellman, Diffie, and Merkle suggested a *two-key* system. One key, the private key, is kept secret as with a traditional encryption system but the other key is made public. Anyone could use the public key to send a message but only the owner of the secret key could decipher it. This eliminated the need for a coding machine, which had to be guarded.

"To now decipher a secret message, *brute-force* could be used. This is like attempting to get someone's phone number by trying all possible combinations. This method will work but only in a very long time.

"When you are getting money from an ATM you are using encryption. Entering your PIN begins a key exchange to transfer the money. Without encryption, your bank account and much more couldn't be kept safe. Despite its evil reputation, encryption *is* good for it makes things safer even if it is sometimes used by bad people."

"Like those we must keep from our records," Lindsay said, and I could have hugged her.

"Exactly so," Randy said, with a big smile.

"Would you have the time to inspect our computer system?" Lindsay pleaded.

"I'll *make* the time," Randy said, staring hard into her beautiful face.

I admit it. Though her invitation was what I had prayed for, I couldn't help feeling jealous.

Chapter 22

We were invited to visit the Agency's office on the following Saturday when it was closed. This pleased Randy since he preferred to have few people around while he did his business.

The Agency's office was on West 57th Street, down the street from Carnegie Hall. It consisted of a conference room, an office with space for a half-dozen workers, and four private offices for interviewing and counseling.

As we sat in the conference room, Lindsay detailed the Agency's operations. Though bored by her presentation, Erika and I managed to glow with interest and admiration while Randy spoke with their computer expert.

We had arrived at ten. At eleven, Erika stated that she had reserved a lunch reservation for us at Eleven Madison Park, an American/French restaurant on 24th Street. It was far enough away in Manhattan's congested traffic to take lengthy travel time. We would also need to find a parking garage.

Lindsay readily agreed. Though new, this restaurant was already considered one of Manhattan's jewels and Saturday reservations were hard to make.

Randy said that he had a large breakfast and preferred to continue working to finish the job and not have to return. This move had been planned. Alone in the office, he could do what he wanted without having to answer awkward questions.

At the restaurant, Erika ordered dishes that took time to prepare. It was nearly two o'clock before we returned, sated and smiling. Randy smiled too, having apparently succeeded.

On the ride back to Greenwich, he tossed a small USB drive in my lap.

"Third-nine gigabytes, everything that the Agency has on their server is in your lap," he said, carelessly, implying that the task had been child's play for him.

"My brother's adoption was done in the paper-work era. What if his record isn't on their computer?" I asked.

"It was. The last of their ancient records was digitized four months ago. You lucked out," Randy replied.

That our luck continues, I prayed.

Chapter 23

I silently returned the USB drive to Randy. He knew that I was grateful so there was nothing for me to say. Nor was Erika talkative. She is sensitive enough to know when silence is best. From the front seat, Abram spoke a few minutes later.

"Did you have a good trip?" he asked, as the car entered Connecticut.

"Very good, and thank you," I said.

"For what?"

"For all that you've done for Erika and me. You've gone way beyond your job," I replied.

Abram didn't reply. We had known each other for years and none was needed. Abram dropped Randy off at his house.

"I'll let you know as soon as I find something," Randy promised, squeezing my hand.

I simply nodded. Now too, there was nothing for me to say. Once in Erika's bedroom, I lay on the chaise lounge and moped.

"Randy will find him," Erika said, supportively.

But we both knew that was more hope than certainty. My brother's ancient file might, accidentally, not have been digitized, or his record could have been misplaced. Now, twenty years later, he might be lost to finding.

I nodded and sprawled—waiting. I jumped up as my phone's Taylor Swift ringtone filled the room.

"When will you be home?" Melody, my oldest sister, asked, in an annoyed tone.

"I don't know, soon probably. I'm at Erika's," I replied.

"We *must* talk."

"Uh huh."

"When will that be?" Melody persisted.

"Look, I'll be home when I'm home!" I said, angrily, and hung up.

Erika stared. We both knew that losing one's self-control is never a good move.

"What was that about?" Erika asked.

"It was Melody. I'll apologize to her," I said.

But being tense, I didn't shut up and my secret burst from me. I would have told Erika eventually just not then.

"Melody suspects that I'm pregnant," I said.

"Are you?" came her logical question.

After a lengthy silence, I simply nodded.

Chapter 24

Erika's response was the word that I had been trying to break myself of using: "Huh!"

I smiled weakly.

"Was the pregnancy planned?" she asked.

"No, it was an accident."

"Do you plan to keep the child?"

"Yes."

"And Randy is the father?"

"Of course!"

"If you ever need help...'

"Thanks."

Her offer wasn't a surprise since we had long been like sisters.

"Do your parents know?"

"Not yet. I've told only Randy and now you. I was waiting for the best moment to tell them."

"There probably isn't one," Erika said.

I nodded agreement and, after a brief silence, got up.

"I'd better get home and face the music," I said.

"It may not be so bad," Erika said.

"Maybe not but it'll be a shock though I'm certainly not the first Mormon unwed mother."

Erika nodded. The father of another of our friends, Missy Rheese, is a Mormon Bishop. She already had one baby and was pregnant at the time of her marriage, in a civil ceremony a year earlier.

Abram drove me home. Walking through the door, I was unsure whether to face Melody or my parents first, I felt prepared for anything except what I saw.

Seated on the living room sofa were sixteen-year-old Melanie and two friends. They were so intent on what they were reading that they hadn't noticed my entrance into the room.

Before them, on the coffee table, lay a collection of small containers. I picked one up. It read "Zombie Cure" and contained directions following a person's "zombification." Another container was in the shape of a toaster pastry. The last was circular, black, and spiked. They're stylish pill containers, I told myself.

My mind seemed not to be working well. What pills are most popular with students? I asked myself. The ADD drugs or, in street lingo, *speed*. Was Melanie taking it or, even worse, selling it? A felony drug arrest isn't something that anyone needs.

"*What are these*?" I asked firmly, though feeling afraid to learn.

Chapter 25

My mind continued racing as the girls stared at me like I was crazy. No, the pills aren't *speed* but worse! They're *ecstasy* or *crystal meth*, I thought. But the truth wasn't shocking.

"Sit down! You shouldn't get stressed now of all times," Melanie said, in an almost maternal fashion.

"Huh!" I replied, repeating the same dumb word that I had sworn against using.

"You're selling drugs!" I burst out.

"Sit down!" Melanie repeated, and I did.

"Do you want water or juice?" she asked.

I shook my head, feeling unable to speak. I seemed to be in shock. Melanie showed me what the girls had been reading and its title explained everything: "Choosing Your Best Birth Control Pill." I calmed down, and felt ashamed.

"I'm so sorry but when I saw the pill boxes I went crazy. I thought that maybe you'd been pulled into selling drugs while I was in Berlin," I said.

"That doesn't say much for my ability to choose friends. They'd never touch drugs. They bought these pill boxes for me. Aren't they gorgeous?" Melanie asked.

Her friends stared at me coldly.

After introductions, Lucy said, with a smile, "Well, older people *are* an odd species," and the atmosphere relaxed.

"Are you on the pill?" she asked me.

I was taken aback by her question. Talking about birth control in my family's living room hadn't been something that was done. Obviously, there had been big changes while I was away.

"We rely on condoms," I said, honestly.

"Condoms reduce sensation. You won't enjoy sex as much," Debbie asserted, with the tone of an expert.

"I haven't complained not has my partner," I said.

I felt my cheeks redden. Without meaning to, my tone seemed that of a 1910 school teacher. The conversation was outside my comfort zone.

"You won't have to worry for a while," Joanne added.

I gave her a puzzled look.

"Melanie said you're pregnant."

Chapter 26

Knocked out in Round One, I thought. I had initially hoped to keep my pregnancy secret until I "showed" but it now seemed that everyone knew. If Melanie strongly suspected, then so must my parents and Melody. Maybe even my baby sister, Claudine. It had been a weird day, I mused, in what must have been the understatement of the year.

I admitted the truth to the girls, feeling too worn out to fudge or lie. What difference did it make if they learned now or when plumpness made my situation obvious? None.

Suddenly, I became the child and they the mother. What could they do? Were there errands they could perform for me? I thankfully refused but to meet their desire to be helpful, I asked them to research popular baby names.

"We'll throw you a baby naming party," Joanne insisted, and I couldn't refuse. Then, pleading fatigue, I went to my room and lay down, trying to decide what else I needed to share with my family.

Some matters I eventually would: the existence of my brother once I found him, and Lena's illness. But she would not want me to reveal it while there was still hope though my parents had seemed suspicious.

I lay my hands over my belly, seeking the movement that was not yet there. Then, cuddling with the fantasy of Randy beside me, I fell asleep and did what my mother considers unpardonable: not appearing for dinner.

I had been so tired when I lay down that I hadn't completely closed the bedroom door. When I awoke, I found my parents seated beside me.

"We heard that you were sleeping. I brought your dinner," my mother said, and I could see that she had been crying.

Bringing the food was an excuse since we had to talk. Neither she nor I knew how to begin but my father did. Being a lawyer, dealing with touchy personal situations is second-nature to him.

"We visited Lena and she told us of her illness," he said softly.

I nodded, and my eyes teared.

"'Pray one for another, that ye may be healed,'" my mother said, the words of the Apostle James.

So as the food grew cold, we prayed. The Santeria Gods are not jealous, Mother Marie had once told me. Lena needed all the help that she could get.

Chapter 27

Being pregnant is like becoming a child again. It is especially this when living with the family that you grew up with. My sharing of chores was over, and no one could do enough for me. Nor was I criticized for failing inflexible rules, like arriving on time for meals. Finally, I put my foot down.

"I'm normally pregnant, not catastrophically disabled. I can still do things for myself!" I insisted.

Though my parents gave in, they still granted me privileges. So be it, I told myself. Whatever makes them happy.

Randy phoned and said that his parents took the news of their upcoming grandchild well. His doctor-father treated it like a normal medical event and hadn't referred to Randy and I not being married. Whatever his mother's real feelings, she had been calm and left them unsaid. He added, casually, that he had found my brother.

Wealthy Greenwich is not a good place to seek an adoptable baby. According to the Agency's files, only one baby from Greenwich had ever been placed for adoption. He had my birth date and the adoptive parents had lived in New York City.

"They must be rich, living in The Dakota," Randy said.

I had been taken on a school tour of The Dakota as a Barnard College freshman. The apartment building had overwhelmed me. Its architectural style is officially labeled German Renaissance but it has also been called Brewery Brick and Middle-European Post Office.

Its construction was completed in 1884, by the same firm that designed New York City's Plaza Hotel. It was called The Dakota because at that time the area was thinly inhabited and considered as far from civilization as the Dakota Territory.

The building is square and built around a central courtyard. It has high gables, deep roofs, and many panels and balconies. High above its 72nd Street entrance, the figure of a Dakota Indian stands watch.

The apartments have up to twenty large rooms. Some are nearly fifty feet long and many ceilings are fourteen feet high.

Among the famous tenants was the former Beatle, John Lennon, who was murdered in 1980, and the composer, Leonard Bernstein.

"It's a rare place," Randy commented, after I shared these facts.

"Does his family still live there?" I asked.

"No."

"Where are they?"

"I don't know. They seem to have disappeared," he said.

Chapter 28

"People don't just disappear," I said, feeling disappointed.

The task which had originally seemed straightforward—to gain access to the files and discover my brother's address—had become an entirely new ball game. And at a time when my energy decreased and my mood swings increased by the day!

"The Blakes seem to have. I got many 'hits' when I Googled their names but none had their right ages. I did try!" Randy insisted.

"I know that you did, It's just with all that's going on I had hoped for this to be over with quickly," I said.

"I'm still digging. There might be a forwarding address in the apartment house records. Some files probably aren't digitized and are in storage. If we could see them..."

I had a sudden idea. The Dakota building was now a co-op.

"Is the apartment that the Blake's lived in for sale?" I asked.

"I don't know. I'll have to check," Randy replied.

"Do it. That could be our opening. A potential buyer wanting to research the apartment's history to learn if problems had caused the past owners to move."

"They'd never believe us," Randy said.

"No, but they would if the inquiry came from Erika's father," I said.

I sensed Randy's smile.

"Who will we be this time?" he asked.

"Friends of the billionaire buyer's daughter. We're helping her decide on her Manhattan pied-a-terre," I said.

"I'll check if the apartment is available. You know, with the money we got in Berlin, we might have enough to buy it ourselves," Randy said.

"We're not spending that kind of money until you create a startup like Google," I said.

"I should be so lucky."

"You're as smart and creative as any of their founders," I said, firmly.

Chapter 29

Mental reminders can pop up anytime so I wasn't surprised by my thought after hanging up: that I hadn't told Lena of being pregnant. But this was excusable: coping with her life-threatening illness would require all her emotional reserves. I had to support her and had others to support me. I phoned Erika.

"I need another favor," I said.

"Ask! My life is dull when you're not around," she said, in a high-spirited tone.

"Randy found the couple that adopted my brother."

"That's great!" she interrupted.

"Except that they seem to have disappeared. He can't find them but is still looking."

"Didn't they leave a forwarding address where they last lived?"

"They last lived at The Dakota in Manhattan."

"I've seen the building. It's unique."

"Yes, well, Randy has hacked into its records but the older ones haven't been digitized. He's checking with realtors to see if the apartment is vacant and for sale. If so, a potential buyer might be able to see its records, to check if there had been problems in the past. The manager would never believe our interest in buying the apartment but he would your father's."

"He might actually buy it," Erika said.

"Huh?"

The word burst from me, this habit being harder to break than I thought.

"My dad is spending a lot of time on Wall Street and has talked of getting a City apartment where he can stay over. Manhattan has become a startup hub and a great place to make business contacts. I'm glad that you asked. When will you know about the apartment?" Erika asked.

"It shouldn't take Randy long. I'll call you soonest," I promised.

"Soonest" was ten minutes later.

"It *is* available. They're asking four-million-seven-hundred-thousand-dollars but you might be able to talk it down," I said.

"I wouldn't bother. It's low enough," Erika said.

I said nothing. Compared to her forty-million-dollar home, this apartment's cost wasn't worth a second thought.

Chapter 30

The Dakota apartment that we visited was one of the smaller ones. It had two bedrooms, separate living and dining rooms, a den, and a full-size kitchen. The floors were inlaid with mahogany and oak.

We had dressed demurely, as befit a billionaire's daughter and her friend. Randy, who was introduced as Erika's father's business intern, scanned the written records while we toured the apartment.

Randy found that living at The Dakota is no simple matter. The building's rules were long and detailed and we came afoul of them even before entering the building.

Abram had driven us into the City, intending to park in the building's driveway and accompany us inside. But the building had complicated rules governing chauffeurs. Only cars belonging to tenants could enter the driveway, and the doorman would not permit chauffeurs to wait there or loiter in the lobby. We resolved this dilemma by having Abram park in a garage and we walked to the building.

Such building rules were familiar to me. When working as a babysitter, I was permitted to use the passenger elevators *only* when accompanying a child. Domestic employees and messengers had to use the service elevator.

While seated in the vacant apartment, listening to the realtor's sales talk and noshing cookies (which looked suspiciously like Pepperidge Farm), Erika read the building's rules before passing them to me. One, that residents use only firewood that is provided by the building, struck me as being extreme but I said nothing. I wasn't the buyer.

Randy was still reading the records when Erika, Abram, and I left the building. We had made plans to meetup at a nearby restaurant, Jacob's Pickles, when he was finished. I turned toward Erika.

"Well?" I asked.

"Great views and the public areas–courtyard, elevator, staircases, brass and ironwork–are spit and polish. The security is adequate though not nearly as good as at our house."

"Do you think your dad will buy it?" I asked.

"Yes, he will," Erika said, firmly.

She had made up his mind.

Chapter 31

It was a short walk to Jacob's Pickles. We ambled in silence until Erika spoke.

"It's turned lousy," she said.

Erika had assumed, as she often does, that I had read her mind but not this time.

"What's turned lousy?" I asked.

"The Greenwich housing market. Many houses can't nearly be given away," she said.

Greenwich, just thirty miles from New York City, has long enjoyed its reputation as a bastion of wealth, known for its concentration of hedge funds, gentleman farms, and waterfront estates with yachts in back.

"Oh," I sniffed.

Years before, I had inherited a house from a distant relative. It will become mine when I reach twenty-one. Despite my family's years of poverty caused by my father's illness, adequate housing had never been an issue for us. Our home was owned by an ancient family trust which allowed us to live there rent-free. Without this benefit, we might have lived in a camper.

"It's been a soft market for at least five years. There simply aren't as many people willing to pay millions for a house, even one in Greenwich," Erika said.

"Oh."

"It's not just the price. What it comes down to is, as realtors' stress, 'location, location, location.' Downtown houses still sell quickly regardless of their price. People want to live close to shopping and the train station. Even in horse country, walkability counts."

I nodded as we reached Jacob's Pickles.

There was a massive line inside but we were seated instantly.

"The owner was told that we'd be coming. My dad and he have friends in common," Erika said.

The super-wealthy have their own social class and billionaires usually get what they want, I thought, but didn't say. It would have been nasty and Erika and her father had always been good to me.

Abram demanded a table against the wall, food being secondary to security for him. He never ate on the job except when he had been working many hours and Erika insisted. Then, he would order only a sandwich, eating with one hand while his other rested on the pistol under his jacket. Abram had been Erika's bodyguard for years.

"It's Southern comfort food," Erika said, as the waiter seated us.

I shuddered, these words spelling poison to a vegetarian. But I managed to find things to eat on the long menu. I ordered the Black Peppercorn Seared Salmon, Black Eye Peas, and Sour Green Tomatoes. Erika had the Catfish Tacos, and Abram nibbled on biscuits. Randy entered the restaurant soon after our food arrived.

Chapter 32

Randy barged into the restaurant full steam ahead. As the headwaiter put up a restraining hand to stop him, Randy pointed toward us, said something, and came over. He spoke even before sitting down.

"I found the family's forwarding address but it won't help," he said, before catching his breath.

I caught his arm and pulled him onto the chair next to mine.

"Why not?" I asked, calmly.

I wasn't greatly disappointed. Most twenty-year-old forwarding addresses are out of date.

"The address was good but..."

Randy was having a hard time spitting it out. I said nothing, knowing that he would soon explain what he meant. I waited patiently as Randy fidgeted, first at his collar and then rearranging his chair.

Finally, I gave up. It had been a long morning and I was exhausted. Pregnancy wears you out.

"Randy, what is it?" I asked, softly but determinedly.

At that moment, the waiter arrived and asked for Randy's order. After taking a long time reading the menu, he looked up, nodded toward me, and said, "I'll have what she has."

It was a safe choice. I had been hassling him about his lousy diet which matched those of the other pizza/snack food/soda gorging computer students at Yale.

It was obvious that Randy didn't want to say what he had discovered and that's what I said.

"What is it that you don't want to tell us?" I asked, in a spit-it-out-now tone.

"They're all dead. At least that's what everyone thinks," Randy said.

Just as when Lena revealed her deadly illness, it took a moment for my brain to understand what Randy had said. Erika understood more quickly and asked the logical question. Abram's eyes had stopped scanning the room and bore into Randy's face.

"Why are you uncertain they're dead?" Erika asked.

At this question, Randy seemed to recover himself. He looked toward her, then toward me, and then at Abram before speaking.

"Because their bodies were never found," he answered.

Chapter 33

We stared at Randy.

"That makes no sense," Erika said.

"Start at the beginning," I suggested, and Randy did.

"The Blake family lived in the Dakota for twelve years before moving to Washington, D.C. That's where their trail ends."

"You spoke of bodies," I said.

"The *Washington Post* reported a fire at their home. No bodies were found and that's where their trail goes cold. To buy an apartment at The Dakota, one must supply financial information: a social security number, bank references, and more. I tracked them all but none were active after the fire. It's as if the Blakes disappeared."

"Or had never existed," Abram said.

We looked toward him. His comment was unusual since he had never joined in our conversations before.

"What do you mean?" Erika asked.

Abram again scanned the room before replying.

"The Blake's identities could have been false or they might have needed to go into hiding after the fire. With or without the aid of a government," Abram explained.

"Why?" I asked.

"That's a good question," Abram answered.

He resumed scanning the room to indicate that he had nothing more to say. Neither did the rest of us and we concentrated on eating until leaving the restaurant. We were similarly quiet in the car back to Greenwich.

"What's next?" I asked Randy, as we approached his home.

"I have no idea. I'll raise their disappearance with my professor. Maybe we could make finding them a class project," Randy said.

"You're kidding," I said.

"Of course, but I'll ask him in general terms. He might think of something. Let me worry about it. You have enough on your plate," Randy said, leaning over and kissing me.

Chapter 34

"We can only wait for what Randy finds," Erika said, in a sympathetic tone.

I nodded, closed my eyes, and leaned back in the seat.

"You must take care of yourself, for the baby too," she added.

As I began to doze, she took my hand. When the car stopped at my house, I yawned and stretched.

"Call me," Erika said.

"I will."

No one seemed home when I entered so I went directly to my room and lay down. But unwelcome thoughts intruded and napping didn't take hold. I shrank from telling Lena that her son was dead. This would create new pain even as she confronted her own mortality. I felt his loss even though never having known him.

At that moment, when I most needed a mother, she walked in.

"I was thinking about you," I said.

My adoptive mother, who had been my real mother for all my life, sat beside me on the bed.

"I wasn't expecting to be a grandmother so soon," she said.

"I wasn't expecting to be a mother so soon," I said.

We both laughed.

"Would you prefer a boy or a girl?" I asked.

"A boy would be a change for our family but it wouldn't matter. I've been blessed with my daughters," she replied.

I felt content, leaned back, and closed my eyes.

"Do you plan to marry?" my mother asked.

"Would it bother you and dad if we didn't right away?"

"Whatever you do will be fine with us."

"We will marry but I haven't yet gotten comfortable with the idea of being pregnant."

"It'll grow on you," my mother said.

We both laughed again as I thought how odd it was that my unwed pregnancy, which is forbidden by the Mormon religion, had served to bring my family closer.

Chapter 35

Randy phoned two hours later though he knew better. My mother's ban against taking phone calls during meals was another of her Godly commandments. But apparently being pregnant permits flexibility since when I took the call she only smiled.

"We're at dinner," I said quickly, with an apologetic glance toward her.

"I'm sorry but it's important," Randy said.

"You found?"

I didn't want to spell it out since my family didn't yet know about my brother.

"Not yet, but Borya just called. He's arriving in New York tomorrow, with a delegation to meet the president-elect. We're invited to dinner."

Borya, a Russian general, is my great uncle. We had first met in Berlin a month earlier. Randy, an acknowledged computer genius, had already been offered college scholarships by America's FBI and Germany's BND (Bundesnachrichtendienst, the Federal Intelligence Service of Germany).

Borya had invited Randy to attend college in Moscow, and wanted to hire me too. All our expenses, including an apartment, would be paid by the Russian government. Randy would be guaranteed a highly paid job after graduation.

Borya, whose nickname is Lucifer, was charming. But as I had told Randy, "I didn't study in Europe to return to America as a Russian spy."

Randy considered my statement over-the-top but he tends toward innocence.

"Are we going to the dinner?" Randy asked.

"Of course. We'll talk later," I replied, and hung up.

"What's up?" Melody asked.

"My great uncle, Borya. He's part of a Russian delegation that is meeting with Trump. He arrives tomorrow and has invited Randy and me to dinner."

"Will it be at Trump Tower?" she asked, excitedly.

"Maybe. I don't know."

"Could you get us invited?"

I thought for a moment. Having others around would lighten the mood of our meeting. I feared that Borya would press his offers and our second refusal could be tense. He has a cat-like smile that frightens people.

I made a mental note to call Vladimir, my biological father in Berlin, for advice. He is a former Russian general and knows how they think.

"I'll see what I can do," I said.

Vladimir's advice was brief and reassuring: "Hear Borya out. Despite his nickname, he is not satanic. Family is important to Russians and he would never bring you harm. He respects firmness and considered argument so speak freely."

I intended to.

Chapter 36

Since Borya extended the invitation to Randy, it was for him to accept. When he did, he asked if my sisters could come too. Borya replied that he would welcome meeting them, and that we needn't worry about transportation. He would send a car to pick us up and return us home.

Excitement ruled when my sisters learned and their instant worry concerned what they should wear. I said "whatever" but they wouldn't hear of it and we went shopping the next morning. Borya wouldn't notice their clothes. His issues were with Randy and me.

To my sisters' disappointment, the dinner wasn't at Trump Tower. Instead, we were driven to Le Bernardin, which is widely considered the best French restaurant in Manhattan.

We traveled into Manhattan in a limousine with diplomatic plates and Russian flag flying. This sight was the gossip of our neighbors for days.

Le Bernardin is expensive and has service to match. An extra touch, which I've seen nowhere else, is the small hammock provided for your purse.

Borya arrived with his bodyguard soon after the waiter seated us. He smiled broadly, shook hands with Randy and squeezed his shoulder familiarly, and kissed mine and my sisters' hands. Within moments, his style had won us over.

During moments of small talk, Borya described the President-elect: "a charming, funny man, with more warmth than people think." His impression of the Trump family was equally complimentary.

The others looked happy but I remained suspicious. This ingrained attitude may come from my lingering sense of rootlessness at being adopted. What Borya revealed was common knowledge. He had yet to make his move. This came as we snacked on dessert.

"Would your sisters like to visit Trump Tower?" Borya asked.

He might as well have asked if they would like to meet Justin Bieber.

Chapter 37

I asked Randy to accompany my sisters as "chaperone." He obliged, after a brief stare. Melody is four years older than him but Randy had gotten the message: I wanted to speak with Borya alone.

He turned toward me as soon as the others were gone.

"It's best that we speak alone," he said.

I nodded and said nothing. Being silent is a good negotiating tactic and that's what we were doing. Though I had known Borya only briefly, I sensed his intricacy and the game we were playing. Part of this was to not put delicate matters into words so that pretense could be maintained.

Borya tried to avoid embarrassing you with too much knowledge. When he told you something, you knew that it was for a purpose, and to express his confidence in you.

Borya and Vladimir shared qualities that had made them successful. They could acknowledge the impossibility of a mission while making it seem possible. This would scare away the timid but challenge the bold.

One might respond agreeably, or sense the danger in continuing the conversation and back off. They would give you that option, without melodrama. Just a soft voice speaking so meanderingly that a listener would have nothing worthwhile to quote.

You would let him know that you were interested by simply continuing the conversation. If you were afraid and wanted out, you could pick up a thread that led you out of that conversation's maze.

"What I said in Berlin was true: you have rare qualities as an agent," Borya said.

He was referring to a meeting at the Federal Intelligence Service of Germany during which he had lauded my abilities ("Margaret is a freak of nature. She has been a master of deception operations since she was thirteen...one of the breed of Americans who can battle dirtier than their enemy...a street fighter with a big set of Russian balls.")

I said nothing.

"May I call upon you for service?" Borya asked.

"America is my country. I won't work against it," I said, agreeing indirectly.

"I would never ask that but our nations occasionally share the same interest. We were allies in the Great War."

The Great War is the Russian term for World War II.

"Being pregnant crimps one's style," I said.

"Pregnancy passes and whatever help you need will be provided."

I leaned back in my chair.

"Uncle, I'm sure that you have many talented people and I've already been offered a job. Why do you want me?" I asked.

Then, with an impish smile, I removed my wallet from my purse and flashed my Texas Reserve Deputy Sheriff badge. My appointment had made by the Austin Sheriff. He offered me a job after I graduate from college.

Borya fingered the badge admiringly before handing it back.

"He recognized your nature, the only work that will satisfy you."

"What's that?" I asked, feeling intrigued.

"Wearing a gun on your hip, and being a hunter."

Hearing these words, I would have fallen had I not been seated. For I *knew*, without any doubt, that Borya was correct.

Chapter 38

"Can I help in any way?" Borya asked, in a kindly tone.

"I can't think of anything," I responded.

But I touched his hand, feeling grateful.

"Nothing?" Borya asked.

His expression indicated that he knew more than he had said.

"Lena phoned Vladimir and told him of her...condition," Borya said.

We were no longer negotiating but I said nothing.

"He offered to find her the best European doctor but she's satisfied with her's. He also offered to help find your brother."

Borya sat silently as my eyes filled with tears. I dried them with the napkin before speaking.

"We've already discovered some information. My brother was adopted by a family named Blake. Randy accessed their adoption agency's file and their records from the Manhattan building where they lived. After leaving Manhattan, they moved to Washington D.C. where the trail goes cold. A fire destroyed their home but no bodies were found and their financial accounts were never used again. Randy is writing software to search for a new lead," I said.

"Washington isn't a far-off jungle. People don't just disappear from there," Borya mused.

I nodded agreement.

"And for so long."

Again, I nodded agreement.

"Would you object if I studied this puzzle too?"

"I'd welcome it. I'll have Randy send you what he has. I'm not sure how much time Lena...we have," I said.

My eyes teared again and Borya took my hand.

"God is merciful. Do not lose hope," he said.

I was so startled by his comment that I couldn't help smiling.

"You're smiling," Borya said, matching my smile with his.

"I wouldn't have expected a Communist to speak of God," I said.

"Communism is gone. Russia is now a capitalist nation with a capitalist God."

Though speaking flippantly, his expression had been serious.

Chapter 39

Our negotiation was over. Borya had asked if he could depend on me for service and I had agreed. In turn, I could rely on him for help, whatever it was and wherever it was needed. Life is a war in which evil is strong and goodness is weak. We all need allies.

Nothing was written on paper and no court could enforce our pact. Nevertheless, it would bind us until our deaths, which hopefully wouldn't be soon.

Silent, comfortable moments passed. There was no more to say. I sipped water as he sipped wine.

"What will you do now?" Borya asked.

I hadn't considered this. My concern for Lena and pregnancy had fogged my mind.

"I don't know," I said, honestly.

"Rest. You've had trying months," Borya said, supportively.

"Vladimir told you what happened?"

"Everything, in case you needed help. He's designated me your godfather."

"Thank you," I said, and couldn't help smiling.

Everything had been my aiding in the rescue of a kidnapped child in Texas, and rendering justice to a crime boss in Berlin.

Neither was done through wholly legal methods. As Cody, the retired Texas Ranger who worked with us had said, "There is the justice of lawyers and the courtroom, and the justice of The Prophets and of God." Upon hearing this, Vladimir had ordered me to hire him. Cody is his kind of guy.

When Randy and my sisters returned, everyone seemed to talk at once. They hadn't seen President-elect Trump as they hoped but were floored by the antics surrounding Trump Tower. Horseback mounted police, long-gun toting security, and pickets protesting the election result created a circus-like atmosphere.

"If it weren't for Claudine, we never would have gotten in," Melanie exclaimed, hugging her baby sister.

"*Huh!*" I burst out, noting, unhappily, that this shameful speech habit of mine now seemed permanent.

Chapter 40

I asked the expected question.

"*What happened? Ask her?*" Melanie screeched. pointing toward her sister.

But it was Randy who explained, clearly and coherently like the born teacher that he is.

"It was a mob scene. Everyone wanted to get a glimpse of Trump, and into the five-story atrium which is a public space. The line through security was long and I didn't think that we'd make it until Claudine saved the day.

"Barron, Trump's ten-year-old son, walked passed with his mother and guards. When he turned to look at the crowd, Claudine gave him a blazing smile and waved. Barron smiled and waved back. When the guard saw this, he assumed that we were known to the Trump family and let us through but that was the last we saw of them."

Barron's reaction didn't surprise me. Everyone relates to Claudine like that for she is startlingly beautiful. While shopping with her, my mother often gets suggestions from strangers that Claudine should be a child model. My mother raised this possibility but Claudine wasn't interested. "I want to be a detective," she said.

Claudine's attitude didn't surprise me. Like many beautiful people, she is oblivious to her looks. Her prized possession is the complete set of Nancy Drew mysteries which she has been re-reading for years.

"What was the atrium like?" I asked.

"Gorgeous," Melody replied. "It's covered with rose and yellow marble and crowned with a skylight It has a sixty-foot internal waterfall spanned by a suspended walkway with a pedestrian bridge and shops."

Claudine's eyes drooped despite her excitement. It was late and past her bedtime.

"We'd better get going. I'm sorry that I didn't get a chance to see the building," I said.

"You could visit there with me. Would you like to?" Borya asked.

Chapter 41

Though Borya accompanied me, my visit to Trump Tower turned out to be nothing special. I was just another tourist. While he met with a joint Russian-American terrorism study group, I strolled the atrium and waited for him in the café.

For those of you who haven't yet visited Manhattan's newest tourist destination, I'll provide a brief description.

Trump Tower is at 721 Fifth Avenue. To enter the atrium, you must pass through a black gateway, beneath two-foot-high gold letters that spell Trump Tower. The doorman wears a flat-topped, round-brimmed, classic doorman hat. Beneath his coat he wears a black-and-white striped vest, and a bowtie.

Borya left me at the elevator so I never got inside an apartment. He later told me, "Any oligarch would feel comfortable at Trump Tower. It's decorated in dictator style."

What Borya meant is that the building and its furnishings were intended to impress. "Go for big, add much gold, think French, and put your name everywhere. Still, it's a pleasant place," he summarized, and I had to agree.

On the drive home, I had alone time to think. I still hadn't decided whether to return to Barnard. It was seven months before I gave birth. I could complete another semester but to what end? I would still have two years until graduation and couldn't see that. Not with a baby, a dying mother, and a father in Berlin who expected me to help manage his business.

"You must take care of yourself," everyone was telling me, and I decided to do that. After returning home, I did what had become a recent habit: taking a nap. After awakening, my nightmare disturbed me for the rest of the day.

Chapter 42

I neither believe nor disbelieve that dreams can predict the future. I'm not sure even if Freud denied this possibility. According to my best friend, Erika, whose years of therapy have made her my go-to girl on such matters, if what you dream does happen, it is because you expected it. Like when you dream of failing an exam for which you were unprepared.

Still, when my friend, Kimberly, was in jail, her young daughter dreamed that her mother would soon be released. And, against all odds and everyone's expectation, this quickly happened. So you figure it.

That day, my dream was like the usual horror movie that you can't forget: murderous adults speaking of killing an innocent teenager.

There was the same large, bleak house of those movies. Yet here, instead of a barely clothed girl, the prisoner was a boy of about my age. He lay on a bed in a cell-like room, staring upward. Emotionless, as if he were drugged.

I had sneaked into the house while the couple was away. Now, they had returned. I sought to flee but each door that I tried was locked. The last door had a peephole and, as they approached me on the corridor, I peeked in and saw the boy.

I knew that the boy was about to be killed but felt unable to stop them or to escape. I was soaked with perspiration when the ringing of my phone awoke me.

I picked it up, still wrapped in the dream and unable to speak. The voice at the other end seemed familiar but I couldn't immediately place it.

Margaret in Manhattan

"Margaret, is that you?" Olga asked, hesitantly.

As I replied, memories of what we had experienced in Berlin passed through my mind.

Chapter 43

I hadn't expected Olga to contact me so soon. When we last met two months earlier, she was over-wrought–which was understandable.

While a teenager, she had been kidnapped and forcibly impregnated by a baby-selling gang. After a harrowing escape following delivery, she had lived with Vladimir, adopting the name of his daughter who was murdered during a terrorist attack in Moscow. His care and suggestions had healed her.

After rigorous training, Olga became one of Vladimir's most valued employees, working as bodyguard to the rich and famous. Soon after my arrival in Berlin, while acting as my guide and bodyguard, she had told me her mission in life: to render justice to the criminal who kidnapped her, and to regain her twins.

I had helped to accomplish her first task and we had located her twins in New York City. Being familiar with the City, I had vowed to help her when she was ready. Apparently, she now was. We both sought those who were long-lost.

"Did I disturb you?" Olga asked.

"No, you pulled me from a nightmare. I'm glad that you called. Where are you?"

"At the Greenwich station. I'll stay at a hotel."

"No, you won't. You're staying with us. I'll pick you up in ten minutes," I said firmly.

I hadn't cleared this decision with my mother but she welcomes visitors. For her, each person represents a potential convert to the Mormon faith. But she engages them tactfully and stops when sensing resistance.

My mother is also a wonderful cook and willing listener. Moreover, Olga's story would enthrall her though she would be given only its sanitized version. And my father's legal knowledge would come in handy: wrenching stolen children from the parents who brought them up involved complex legal issues.

My mother came in as I was leaving.

"My friend from Berlin just arrived at the Greenwich Station. I invited her to stay here. I hope it's all right," I said.

"There's always room for one more."

"And maybe more than one?" I asked, placing her hand on my belly.

"*Any time,*" my mother said, with a smile.

Chapter 44

Olga looked *good*. Having money and wearing the right clothes does that for you. In Berlin, Randy had hacked the financial records of the criminal (Dieter) that violated her. Using a "hostile takeover" of his laptop, he transferred millions of dollars from Dieter's bank accounts into new, numbered accounts that I had opened.

I gave three million dollars of this money to Olga, as compensation for her suffering and to start a new life. Obviously, she had used part of it on clothes.

We hugged, and I complimented her appearance.

"Dressing well covers how I feel," Olga said, sadly.

I understood. Few mothers need face her situation: having their children torn from them at birth and sold.

The decision confronting Olga rivaled that of the Biblical Abraham. If her children were doing well and their parents were caring, would it be just to tear them from the only home that they had ever known to satisfy her need? A judge might not permit this.

Moreover, which country's laws would apply: German law, where the crime occurred, or American law, where the children now lived. This was not a simple issue.

But these conversations were for later. Just as she had immediately adopted a tour guide attitude when I first arrived in Berlin, I described the sights of Greenwich as we drove along Main Street. Though, because of their differing size, these places aren't comparable apart from both being old.

Margaret in Manhattan

"It's so green, an idyllic small town," Olga said, as we approached the top of Greenwich Avenue.

I felt pleased by her comment. Greenwich was my home, and maybe that of my future family too.

While stopped at a light, I heard something and turned toward Olga. She was crying.

Chapter 45

After the car behind us honked, I pulled over and double-parked. Finding parking on Main Street is often impossible.

Olga's tears became a river. I handed her a packet of tissues and waited. A minute later I saw flashing lights from a police car behind me. The officer came over, rapped on my car's window, and I lowered it.

"I recognized your car. Is something wrong, Margaret?" asked Sergeant Alamo, an old family friend.

"My friend just arrived from Germany. She's having a meltdown and I wanted to give her a few minutes before going home," I said.

"Can I help?"

"No, I'll move on. But thanks for asking."

"No trouble. Give my regards to your family."

Sergeant Alamo returned to his car and drove off.

"You know him," Olga said, as she dried her eyes.

"He babysat me," I replied.

"It's good to have police like that," she said.

"All OK?" I asked.

"For now, I've been crying a lot. I'm trying to hold together."

My whole family was home when we arrived, assembled in the living room and awaiting introduction.

Margaret in Manhattan

"Where's she sleeping?" asked Claudine, the youngest.

Young kids are most fearful of losing their space.

"In my room. I'm using a sleeping bag," I assured her.

"No, I'll go to a hotel," Olga instantly objected.

"We wouldn't hear of it. You're staying here. Margaret told us how much you helped her in Berlin," my mother insisted.

I didn't remember saying this but behaving courteously is another of my mother's Godly commandments.

"Dinner is at six. Maybe you'll want to nap till then," my mother added.

Olga agreed and I showed her to our room. Upon returning downstairs, I pulled my parents aside.

"Can we speak alone for a few minutes?" I asked.

I felt they should learn Olga's experiences, to better understand if she had another meltdown.

Chapter 46

I sat with my parents in my father's home-office. Though possessing the thick walls common to 19th century structures, my father had its door especially sound-proofed to ensure that his legal conferences remained private. They sat on the sofa and I sat on a wing chair facing them.

"Olga began crying in the car. She's in a bad way," I said.

"I noticed," my father said.

This didn't surprise me. Not much gets by him.

"She's been through a lot. Nine years ago, while a college student in Berlin, she was kidnapped, imprisoned, and forcibly impregnated by a baby-selling gang. She escaped after giving birth but it was a harrowing experience."

I stopped speaking, wanting to give my parents time to fully grasp what I said.

"She spent the next two years living with Vladimir and regaining her courage. Olga is not her birth name. She adopted it after vowing to forget her past and begin a new life. She was one of Vladimir's most valued employees, working as a bodyguard to the rich and famous.

"While in Berlin, Randy and I helped find the criminal who violated her. We also discovered the location of her twin sons. They live in New York City and Olga has come to see how they're doing and possibly to reclaim them.

"She's unsure what to do and this decision is eating her up. If they're well, would it be right to tear them from the only parents they've known? Yet, she is their mother and their current parents' purchase of them was illegal.

"Moreover, which country's law governs the children: German law, where the kidnapping happened, or American law, where they now live? It's a mess."

"Does she have a lawyer?" my father asked, quickly.

"No, and that's another problem. I was hoping that you would represent her. She has money and could pay your fee," I pleaded.

My mother turned toward my father.

"You couldn't accept payment. You'd be doing God's work," she said.

"*Yes*, I'll help her, and *no*, I won't accept payment," my father said.

"*Bless you both*," I said softly, and began crying.

Being pregnant had made me more emotional.

Chapter 47

When Olga came downstairs, my mother treated her like an ill, fragile child.

"This is now your home. Just ask for whatever you need," she instructed her.

With that, dinner turned into our usual with food taking second place to conversation not that we scrimp on eating. But Olga ate little. Food wasn't on her mind.

After dinner, my father invited her into his home office. Since the legal rule of confidentiality is violated if outsiders are present, I had to remain outside. Olga described their discussion afterward.

She had gratefully accepted his offer of legal representation. He told her that her situation was unique and he would have to research legal precedent. He also said that he had a contact in the Justice Department that he might call upon and she agreed to this. She signed the required document hiring him and handed over his requested fee of one dollar. This made their professional relationship binding.

Olga looked more relaxed after their meeting, and I said this.

"Loneliness kills. I no longer feel alone," she said.

Once in our room and free from the prying ears of my sisters, I questioned her.

"What have you discovered about your sons?" I asked.

"They've been named Brian and Jacob. Their parents are doctors with large practices. When not in school, the kids are cared for by a Swedish au pair named Kristina.

"Per their pediatrician's records, which I had hacked, both children are healthy. One of Vladimir's New York agents has photographed the boys."

Olga removed a manila envelope from her briefcase and spread photos on the bed. The children were handsome and resembled her: all had same blond hair and facial bone structure. No one would doubt their mother's identity, which is what I said.

"That makes it even more painful if I must leave without them," Olga said.

"What's your next step?" I asked.

"To see but not speak with them while they're at the Central Park Zoo. They go there every Saturday morning. It's apparently a favorite place. Will you come with me?"

"I wouldn't miss it," I replied.

Chapter 48

That night, Olga's sleep was tormented and so was mine. Being pregnant takes getting used to, both physically and mentally. While tossing in the sleeping bag, I heard Olga moan. But things usually look better in the morning, I told myself, and they did.

We took the Metro-North train from Greenwich into Manhattan. I didn't want to battle the heavy traffic driving into Manhattan and near impossibility of finding convenient parking once there. Few things scare me but driving in Manhattan does.

Our hardest task would be to observe the children close-up without being noticed. We had dressed the part, wearing wrap-around sunglasses and the usual clothes of young tourists: jacket, jeans, and sneakers.

A backpack with a Berlin logo hung over my shoulder while Olga carried a sturdy briefcase. Concealed inside, was a miniature video recorder with its lens peeking unnoticeably through a corner.

We knew the children's routine. At precisely 10AM they left the Fifth Avenue apartment building where they lived, walked south two blocks, crossed the street, and entered Central Park. The Zoo was a short walk down a meandering path.

We had been sitting on a bench opposite their apartment house early, since 9:30AM, to be sure not to miss them. But the boys and their au pair had followed their usual schedule. As they walked the two blocks, we followed slowly on the opposite side of the street, not wanting to catch up with them when they crossed.

Margaret in Manhattan

As they entered the park, we let several strolling families separate us. The boys were dressed in easy to follow, identical, red-and-blue jackets.

Their phones were more enticing than the animals that day. Just before the zoo's entrance, the boys seated themselves on a bench and, apparently, began playing a video game. The au pair opened a magazine.

Olga took a small pad from her jacket pocket and began writing. When finished, she turned toward me, smiled hugely, and showed me what she had written. The note read: "Smile and don't look around. We're being watched."

Chapter 49

I did as Olga instructed. I smiled, and she took my arm and led me away. Only after our backs were to the children, did she speak.

"They might overhear us with a parabolic microphone. I didn't want to take a chance," she said.

"Better safe than sorry," I said, though considering her action to be more than a bit much.

"Their surveillance was good but not perfect. There are at least three of them watching. The boys were centered in their circle," Olga said.

"OK. What now?" I asked.

"Now we follow them. The video recorder has their photos. We can try to identify them later," she said.

I followed her lead. The children were hers and this was her operation. Since they were central to the watchers' attention, all we need do is keep track of the boys. When they moved, so would their surveillance team. We walked a hundred feet and sat on an empty bench.

Several minutes later, a woman seated herself on our bench and began working on a laptop. After exclaiming, "well," she closed the laptop, looked around, and smiled at us. I smiled back as my survival instinct began screaming.

"It's lovely out. There aren't many days like this in Alaska. Where are you from?" she asked.

"Berlin," I replied.

"Wow! I've never been to Europe."

"Neither have we. We're from Berlin, New Hampshire," I said.

Accurate facts provide ammunition to an enemy. Olga had picked up the same dangerous vibes and let me do the talking.

"What's it like in Berlin?" the woman asked.

"It can be cold like in Alaska though Mayor Grenier has described it as 'heaven on earth,'" I replied.

"You don't agree?"

"Maybe it was before the paper industry died. Now, the biggest employer is the prison that opened four years ago. My father works there. Her uncle does too," I said, indicating Olga.

The woman deliberately looked at her watch.

"That's interesting. I'd best get going. Have a pleasant day," the woman said, in a cheerful tone.

When she was out of hearing range, I turned toward Olga.

"What did you make of her?" I asked.

"Her, or the gun she wears in a Flashbang bra holster?"

"I didn't notice."

"You weren't supposed to. She has small breasts and I noticed the outline of the pistol's grip," Olga said.

Chapter 50

"Is Grenier really the Mayor of Berlin?" Olga asked.

"He is according to Wikipedia. We'll seem legitimate if she checks," I replied.

"That was good planning."

"I'm just trying to keep us alive," I said.

We didn't speak again until being seated in of a coffee shop three blocks away. There, my thoughts turned to Olga.

Despite her informal dress, she was the essence of "coolness" with her suave exterior, cynical detachment, and unspoken courage. But, most of all, her lack of self-pity.

If anyone would be expected to lament their life, she would. While a teenager she had been kidnapped, forcibly impregnated, had her newborns sold, and barely escaped with her life. My thoughts returned to her sons.

"Why do they have such big-time protection?" I asked.

"I have no idea. Clearly, the boys must be crucially important to some organization. Even wealthy parents can't afford security like that and doctors aren't in the league of the super-rich. There are more attractive ransom targets in Manhattan."

"So, what now?" I asked.

"Now we check out their parents. And if we could hack into their school records..."

"I'll get Randy onto it," I promised.

"Will he do it?"

"He will. He likes you," I replied.

It's time to get Olga's mind back to ordinary things, I thought.

"You've never been to Manhattan, have you?" I asked.

"No."

"Come, we can go shopping," I said, with a big smile.

This magical word produced the smile that I had hoped. We left the coffee shop and walked down Madison Avenue, admiring the creations in shop windows. Yet Olga's sadness persisted and I wondered if it was only from the loss of her sons.

"Do you have a boyfriend?" I asked, intuitively.

"I thought that I did until he told me otherwise."

"What happened?"

"The usual. He was different from what I thought."

"What is he like?"

"He's ten years older than me, strikingly good-looking and conscious of it. Very conceited and *very* touchy. Always well-dressed but with a touch of calculated disinterest. He's a born actor and it was impossible to get through his defenses,

"I was what he longed for yet also feared: the exciting and unexpected. Unfortunately, I also spelled chaos for his tidy, lonely existence," Olga said.

"What kind of work did he do?" I asked, this typical American question.

"He's assistant to the chief of MAD (Militärishcher Abschirmdienst, Germany's military counter-intelligence), coordinating their activities. Your father warned me against him."

"Is he married?"

"No, he's a womanizer but doesn't really like women. His kindness doesn't extend to the women who love him."

"You're better off without him," I said.

"That's what I decided and what your father told me earlier," Olga said.

We strolled on in silence.

Chapter 51

Even Bergdorf Goodman's great Fifth Avenue store couldn't lift Olga's mood. After a half-hour of wandering through it I gave up trying. We took a taxi to Grand Central Station and caught the next train home.

My sisters were out, my father was in his home-office and my mother was in the kitchen. While Olga napped, I called Randy.

"Olga needs a favor," I said immediately.

"Is she here? You didn't tell me she was coming."

"She arrived unexpectedly yesterday. So, will you?"

"Of course, what is it?"

"What you're best at."

"Making love?"

"What you're second best at. I'll come over and tell you," I said.

"It's *that.*"

"Yes," I replied.

Randy understood. Some matters are too private to discuss over the phone.

Randy was babysitting his toddler sister when I arrived. She was busily giving small stuffed figures a ride on a toy truck and he occasionally put into words what she was doing. "Wow! You're taking baby for a ride."

I hated to interrupt but was prouder of him than I could express. Randy had become a great big brother. He kissed his sister upon leaving her and again when he returned. He even, and this really surprised me, diapered her when needed. That he should behave like this with our children, I prayed.

"Randy must speak with Auntie Margaret now. But if you need me, just call," he said, kissing her before rising to kiss me.

"You're *wonderful*!" I whispered, and hugged him tightly.

"Well, maybe in my better moments," he said, modestly.

"Are your parents around?"

"They're out shopping."

"Good."

Randy knew Olga's situation so I didn't have to explain.

"Her kids are so important that someone is keeping tight surveillance over them and we don't know why. I was hoping that you could hack into their school records to get information."

Randy stared at me momentarily before nodding agreement.

"Olga is a good woman," he said.

"She's the best," I agreed.

Chapter 52

The worst thing is to go off half-cocked. Nothing productive could be done until we had more information: for me, about my brother; and for Olga, about her sons.

Eight-year-old Claudine had quickly latched onto Olga, who willingly watched Disney videos with her. Olga even shared things with her that I hadn't known: events from her normal life before being kidnapped. About this, of course, she said nothing though. Though if she had, it wouldn't have upset Claudine who was an avid reader of Nancy Drew mysteries.

After tolerating three days of silence from Randy, I phoned him.

"Have you found anything?" I asked.

"Something weird. I was about to call you," Randy said.

I waited. Randy's explanations can be slow in coming but are always clear.

"There were identical fragments of private IPs, internet protocol addresses, in some of the messages concerning both your brother and Olga's sons."

"What does that mean?" I asked.

"That their lives are hooked together in some way."

"That makes no sense. My brother was adopted twenty years ago and Olga's sons were stolen years later. How could these events be related?" I asked.

"It beats me but they must be. I could show you the evidence," Randy said.

"No, I believe you. Keep digging."

To relax while waiting, Olga and I had been going on long walks early each morning. They became our time for sharing and bitching. It was then that I shared Randy's conclusion, adding my opinion that it didn't make sense and must be a mistake.

We ended our walks at the local Starbucks, noshing and watching commuters streaming down Greenwich Avenue toward the Metro-North Station. Only when we were comfortably seated did Olga reply.

"No, Randy's finding makes good sense. I think that he's latched onto something far bigger than family matters. Think cell," Olga said.

"Cell, like amoeba?" I asked, and waited.

Olga remained silent. She, like Randy, can't be rushed and I didn't try. Having similar personalities may be why they like each other.

Chapter 53

Life went on while we awaited further information. Meanwhile, my biological mother, Lena, remained involved with her work.

"It helps me ignore fate. There's nothing better for that than managing hospital crises," she said.

During what I feared were her remaining days, I often joined her for lunch, accompanied by Olga or Erika or one of my sisters. Claudine had also latched onto Lena, as if sensing that they both suffered.

"It's harder when you don't speak of pain," Claudine said.

This was apropos of nothing for Lena had just shared a humorous story about a patient.

For a moment, we all stared at Claudine. What she said had been unexpectedly adult.

"You're a very smart little girl," Lena said, softly.

"I've been hurt. I was never little," Claudine said, in the same adult-like tone.

Lena opened her arms and Claudine allowed herself to be hugged, something which she often resisted. By identifying with their child while comforting them, the mother also comforts herself, Erika had once explained. From her years of therapy, she has become my go-to expert on puzzling behavior.

Randy phoned two days later, asking that we come over his house. He was babysitting his sister again, a chore which he loved unlike most siblings.

She was sleeping on the sofa, clutching a large stuffed bear, when Olga and I arrived. Randy covered her with his jacket.

"She likes it. It relaxes her," he explained.

"Because it carries your scent," Olga suggested.

Her comment embarrassed Randy and he quickly removed a folder from his briefcase. We sat on the floor and carefully studied its contents, each page in turn.

"You have *really* smart kids. Look at their scores," he added.

Olga did, and nodded agreement. Both children had achieved better than ninety-nine percent of students their age on the state exams. They could read three years beyond their grade level.

"They might be ready for college at fourteen," Randy added, half-seriously.

Our only surprise came from the bottom of the folder.

"Their parents' photos are last. They're kept for safety, to ensure that only they can pick up the children. I never expected *this*," Randy said, as he spread them before us.

Chapter 54

The boys' parents were Chinese or of another Oriental race. Nor was their name typically Eastern, *Young* had likely been Anglicized from *Yung*. But their sober, well-dressed appearance was unexceptional.

"Why would a Chinese couple buy stolen Caucasian kids when they could easily adopt Chinese kids?" Randy asked.

"Because they were pre-selected and assured of having a healthy mother. Still, one would think that if the mother had a problem conceiving, the parents would have chosen to use the father's sperm," I suggested.

"Western children would be more useful. They would encounter less prejudice and have easier entrée into restricted jobs," Olga said.

"Who thinks about an infant's career?" Randy objected.

"Those who plan ahead," Olga replied.

"Oh, come on!" I said, feeling frustrated. "Did *your* parents consider *your* career before you were born?" I asked.

"Our parents' issues were ordinary. Think of *The Thirty-Nine Steps*," Olga said, her calm tone concealing frustration at our ignorance.

"*The Thirty-Nine Steps*," Olga repeated.

Understanding dawned over my face. *The Thirty-Nine Steps* is an old spy movie describing the unmasking of an undercover cell of German spies in England.

Now I understood Olga's earlier allusion to *cell*. This is a classic espionage technique: secretly planting contacts, spies, and covert supporters in preparation for the day, possibly years in the future, when their services would be needed.

"You're saying that your sons are being groomed to be spies when they're adult. That sounds incredible," I said.

"Not really. Haven't you seen *The Americans*? OK, the TV events are exaggerated. Real spies would quickly flee the country after doing what they did but its premise holds. Who would be considered more loyal than a native born American?" Olga asked.

Who indeed? I thought, and nodded agreement.

Chapter 55

"What do we do now?" I asked.

I had spoken into the long silence that followed Olga's comment. Though sensing that her interpretation was correct, I felt clueless what to do and Randy looked the same. Throwing up his hands in frustration, he asked, "Is anyone hungry?"

His movement caused his baby sister to awaken and he kissed her. "Hungry," she squealed. "Course you are, you're a growing girl." Randy said, kissing her again.

Squeezing his arm, I felt the same warmth that I felt when telling him I was pregnant. He will be a wonderful father to our children, I told myself.

An expression of pain cast over Olga's face, reflecting her sense of what she had missed and might never have.

"What else did you find, Randy?" I asked.

"Nothing exceptional except that the kids are into the martial arts. Each of their files has a permission slip letting them leave school early for that class," he said.

I stared at Randy.

"*What?*" he asked, nervously.

"They've identified us but not you," I said.

Olga looked at me and I sensed that she had the same idea.

"Have you considered studying the martial arts?" she asked Randy.

As Olga's meaning penetrated, fear spread over his face. He had last looked that way when he was thirteen and in danger of being arrested for hacking. My lawyer-father had gotten him off. The case arose from his innocent attempt to help a school-mate.

Though tall and sturdily built, Randy is not a *physical* person. He never got into a fight at school and the idea of sparring terrified him. But he liked Olga and did what we asked though not happily. He turned toward her.

"Maybe you should teach me some basics so I'm not a complete wuss," he said.

Chapter 56

I had two feelings. The first and bigger was that I didn't want Randy to get hurt. Being mostly a thinker, his physical coordination wasn't the best. This was why, at the rare parties that I could coax him to attend, he hardly ever agreed to dance. While dancing, one must synchronize oneself with the music but Randy was most usually in beat with his thoughts.

My second feeling was that it would be good for Randy to become less frightened of physical confrontation even if this is rare for adults. I didn't want our kids to grow up feeling afraid.

I shared my first feeling and kept the second one private. It isn't the kind of thing that one shares with the person concerned.

"Martial arts training teaches to avoid confrontation. If a student gets hurt, the business will be sued. Randy will be OK," Olga promised.

Randy listened uncomfortably. It was like hearing your parents discuss your future.

"But he'll be learning Krav Maga," I said.

Krav Maga is Hebrew for *contact combat* and is the deadly Israeli martial arts. It contains techniques from aikido, judo, and boxing, and specializes in brutal counter-attacks. Variations of Krav Maga are taught in the British Special Action Services (SAS) and America's Marines.

"The psychology is widely taught but not its killing techniques. That's for military people," Olga reassured me.

I accepted her conclusion. She had studied Krav Maga for years.

"Erika has a gym in her house. You could teach Randy there," I suggested.

I spoke with Erika that night and Randy began his training the following day. Abram, Erika's bodyguard, happened to pass the gym and looked in. Thereafter, he helped Olga and this pleased Randy. With Abram present, his training became a male thing.

Chapter 57

Olga wasn't sure how long Randy's training would take. She had initially thought that a week would do but I suggested two. We settled on ten days. Randy wasn't party to this discussion. Since we began dating he had tended to leave decisions to me.

Contrary to our expectations, Randy learned quickly. Though the training was a new experience, he latched onto it as he had to my uncle. Borya, when they met in Berlin, Borya is a Russian general and Americans don't usually meet them.

"He'll never be a killer but you wouldn't want that," Olga whispered to me, as we watched him.

"No, though Abram is taking him for pistol training," I said, in a whisper.

Olga smiled. She was probably also thinking that one can never tell where things lead.

Another surprise was that Randy enjoyed shooting. Abram, like Olga, is a calm, methodical teacher, much like Randy when he tutors.

Randy quickly picked up the basics of safe shooting and became a surprisingly good shot.

"If he wasn't so noticeable, being so tall and handsome, we might make him a spy," Olga said, with a small smile.

"I'd rather that he worked with computers," I objected, though feeling pleased with her description.

"OK, we'll make him into a temporary spy," Olga said.

That evening, we held a party at Erika's home to celebrate Randy's "graduation." There, Olga pronounced him "fit" and Abram pinned on one of his medals. It was a ribbon with three yellow stripes on a blue background.

"It was presented to me 'For Service to The Homeland in The Armed Forces of the USSR,'" Abram explained.

Randy looked proud as we sent him off to war.

Chapter 58

While not a real war there was still danger. Randy's task was to observe the children and possibly befriend them, with the hope that they would drop nuggets of information about their family. It was only that, no heroics and nothing else.

The martial arts studio was located on the Upper East Side, six blocks from where the boys lived. Each weekday their au pair chaperoned them from school to their class. Randy signed up for the same class, explaining that he needed that time because of his college schedule. "Lies should be kept as close as possible to the truth," I had advised him.

Randy suffered in the classes. Not from muscle strain but from boredom. He is an intellectual and having to watch the instructor demonstrate motions and then to endlessly repeat them bored him silly.

"It's driving me crazy," he complained, the evening after his first class.

Erika had Abram drive Randy into the City. While their male bonding helped, it was still a struggle. I tried to make it up to Randy every night.

The other students were standoffish at first but Randy's instinctive clumsiness helped. He became the class pet, the goof-off that everyone likes and wants to help.

It didn't do much for his self-esteem to have kids be so much better than him but it did work. The instructor valued him since an adult's presence confirmed the class's importance. And the students, both girls and boys, treasured his attendance since it wasn't often that they could outdo an adult.

We held our first war conference a week later.

"The boys talk to me and I've exchanged smiles with their au pair," Randy reported.

"Just smiles, I hope," I couldn't help saying.

Randy patted my hand. Olga looked disheartened.

"What do you speak with them about?" she asked.

"Mostly computers. They're building their own with Raspberry Pi and I gave them tips," Randy replied.

"Oh," Olga replied, with a discouraged tone.

"They've invited me to their home to see them," Randy said, with a grin.

Olga's gloom vanished.

Chapter 59

People without friends are often suspicious of human gatherings. Randy is a loner. His only friends were originally mine, those who he had met through me. Technically, they weren't his friends but they liked him and he felt comfortable with them which isn't easy for him.

Thus before Randy "went to war," he had more than the basics of martial arts to learn. He also needed to learn acting, to pick up how to present himself to the boys' family as a naïve, congenial person whose goal was to be helpful–and to get close to their au pair too. I wasn't happy with this but realized its importance: few know more of a family's secrets than their live-in servant.

I had kept Vladimir informed about our activities and he sent someone to help us.

Lee had unique skills and would provide Randy with what he needed. I sat in on their sessions. One shouldn't miss the opportunity to learn from any expert.

"Spies must appear stupid and dull, even cowardly and used to humiliation," Lee began.

Despite his genius-level IQ, Randy's self-esteem isn't high and these words troubled me. They also appeared to trouble him until Lee's next comment.

"But the best spies are highly intelligent and courageous, which is why you'll do a great job. Now, let's get down to business," he said, with a smile, and Randy smiled too.

Lee said that he had formerly worked in the Technical Services Division of the CIA. There, his job had been to produce personal alias documents and gadgets enabling agents to cross hostile borders and to communicate safely.

"I'll provide you with a new identity that you must learn, and new technical skills."

Lee paused for emphasis, to suggest the importance of what he was about to say.

"Vladimir's partner has spoken with his friends in the CIA about Olga's sons. They're concerned and want their apartment 'bugged' but can't do it themselves because of American law.

"Friends do favors for friends and Vladimir regards you as a friend. Because the building's security is so tight, you present the only opportunity. Vladimir asks that you plant the 'bugs.' My job is to teach you how."

Chapter 60

Randy, the father of our yet to be born child, looked pleased. He leaned forward eagerly, being a lover of the latest gadgets. But despite his intellectual brilliance, he lacked street smarts. He had never been in a fight and didn't understand the risk that he was taking.

This wouldn't be a high school tussle. He was volunteering for the big league where people get killed, not suspended. I didn't like it.

"Randy has had no training as a spy. You're going to get him killed. He won't do it!" I stormed.

Olga and Lee stared at me. Randy looked embarrassed but this didn't bother me. It was better for him to be embarrassed than dead, I thought.

"He *won't* get killed," Lee said, soothingly.

"Really! You can guarantee this!" I said, in a tone approaching hysteria.

"No, but hear me out. We know he's a civilian. He'll have whatever is needed to protect him. Whatever is needed!" Lee repeated.

"You also know that what you're asking is illegal," I said.

I feigned a caustic tone despite my having involved Randy in illegal activities in the past. But then *I* had taken the physical risks, keeping him out of the fray. I hated disappointing Olga but preferred that to Randy being dead or in jail.

"No," Lee said.

"No, what?" I asked.

"It won't be illegal."

"How is that?" I asked, in a dubious tone.

"There is now a presidential determination that the activities under investigation present a grave threat to the United States.

"It's no longer a question of the boys' welfare, important though this is. This is now a matter of national security and we'll have whatever help is needed. Meaning, that there will be people willing to sacrifice their life for Randy. If a bullet comes his way, they'll take it for him," Lee said.

Tears filled my eyes as I looked at Randy. He took my hand, looked at Lee, and nodded agreement. Lee rose to get his briefcase and get down to business.

In the silence, my phone rang and I answered it absent-mindedly, having forgotten to turn off the speaker.

"Will I need an injection?" my baby sister, Claudine, asked, in her childish voice.

Her question froze us and aroused our puzzled expressions.

Chapter 61

"*Baby,* what a question to ask. People get injections when they're sick and you're healthy," I replied.

"It said that two million women got injected last year," Claudine said.

"What did?"

"Melanie's magazine."

I immediately understood. Our sister, sixteen-year-old Melanie, had been borrowing fashion magazines that my mother won't let her buy. Though reading since she was four, Claudine lacked perspective on what she had read.

"What you read is about grownup women who hope to look perfect though no one is. It's uniqueness that makes a person beautiful and you're already that. You'll never need those injections."

"Oh. When are you coming home?" Claudine asked, her crisis being over.

"Soon. I'm bringing Randy with me," I replied.

"Oh, good," Claudine said, and hung up.

Randy had become the brother that our family lacked. He kissed her upon arriving and leaving, just as he did his baby sister.

Claudine's call lowered the tension in the room. Now, from his briefcase, Lee retrieved gadgets and placed them on the small folding table that Erika had taken from a closet. Our meetings with Lee would be held in Erika's bedroom, it being more private than my bedroom or Randy's.

At the sight of Lee's electronics, Randy's face lit up like a child's confronting their Christmas presents.

"Ideally, you'd be put through a six-week course covering surveillance, communication, and weapons. But you need know only the basics."

Randy leaned forward expectantly. Being a student was an easy role.

"Always assume that hostile elements are watching. If being followed, don't try to outdistance your pursuer but keep moving at a comfortable pace. An old and still good movie ploy is to watch your reflection in a store window. And wear a cap and reversible jacket. They'll enable you to change colors like a chameleon," Lee said,

"Don't ever focus on a person's superficial appearance. Instead, look for a sudden change in the movement of those around you. You can practice evading surveillance in town, having others try to follow you," Lee concluded.

Randy grinned.

"It sounds exciting," he said.

"It is but if you want to do something really exciting like being an intelligence agent or police officer, you must be cautiously conservative and not cautiously crazy. Any asshole can get an exciting job that kills them," Lee warned.

His grim expression showed that he wasn't joking.

Chapter 62

I sensed that Lee's rank in the CIA had been high. His way of relating and stories reminded me of Vladimir who had been a Russian general. Both tried to avoid embarrassing you with too much knowledge. When they told you something it was for a purpose, as a token of having confidence in you.

While implying that what they asked might be impossible, they also implied that it was doable. This duality would frighten off the timid but challenge the bold. There was no melodramatic statement of mission and call for a volunteer. Just a calm, quiet voice.

"The good agent has decency and common sense. They have great energy but have learned to control their impulses," Lee said.

We listened spellbound as he told us dramatic tales about American spies in the Soviet Union and Asia that he had communicated with and rescued.

"Word of mouth assures privacy. The only good way to avoid being eavesdropped is to pass information during an unpredictable, unannounced walk outdoors. Forget about turning on the shower and speaking in the bathroom like they do in movies. That constant noise can be easily filtered out. Using current technology, we can bug anything almost anywhere but need access to the premises. Which you now have, Randy," Lee said.

From the gadgets on the table, Lee selected a Q-Bug, which he described as being the world's smallest wireless voice transmitter.

Margaret in Manhattan

"It can be placed anywhere and pick up whisper thirty-five feet away. When you phone it, the unit will know that you are its master and you can then call in anytime to listen. There are no rings or click sounds to alarm the target," Lee explained.

He then handed Randy what looked like an ordinary phone,

"This Q-Phone can dial out and operate like any mobile phone. But it also contains a special stealth program which, when activated, lets you know all the phone activity of the user. It will send text messages to your mobile phone that alarm you when the Q-Phone is dialing out or is receiving a call, along with its number. You can then dial in to the Q-Phone and listen to both sides of the conversation.

"I'll give you three of them. Use one when with the boys and say how great it is. If they admire it, you can later make presents of them," Lee said.

"I have an idea. Can you construct a small metal box with attachment screws to contain the Q-Bug?" Randy asked.

"Easily, why?" Lee responded.

"I'll be helping the kids build gadgets using the Raspberry Pi computer module. Other parts must be added–Wi-Fi, power and USB units–to make it functional. I could conceal the Q-bug alongside them," Randy said.

"You were a good choice. Call me when you need a job," Lee said, smiling approvingly.

Chapter 63

Randy's dinner date with the Young family was scheduled for the following Saturday night. Lee met with Randy twice more beforehand but I wasn't present. I had something else to do: my first pregnancy exam.

I hadn't consulted a doctor to confirm being pregnant but didn't doubt this. My over-the-counter pregnancy test in Berlin told me that I was as did my symptoms: gaining weight, becoming nauseous and vomiting, having swollen breasts.

"It's time for your first trimester exam," I was told, by both my biological and adoptive mothers and two friends who had given birth.

For the task of choosing an obstetrician I first asked Lena, my biological mother. Being the manager of a psychiatric hospital, she was tuned into the medical establishment and knew doctors' reputations. Randy's father, a surgeon, might have been an equally good choice but with this matter a girl's mind turns to her mother. Unfortunately, Lena didn't know any obstetricians, good or bad.

"Psychiatrists are in their own little world. I can recommend a great therapist but not obstetrician. It's been a long time since I gave birth and mine didn't ring any bells," Lena said.

My disappointment must have showed for a moment later she suggested, "Why not ask Doctor Cohen?"

"Of course!" I agreed.

Doctor Cohen has been *the* pediatrician in Greenwich since well before I was born. He treated the children in my family, Randy's family, and those of every knowledgeable local parent. Though in his seventies, he was still in practice but with a different nurse. She retired but he carried on.

Having made this decision, Lena and I chatted amiably, trying to avoid the biggest worry on both our minds: her health. It was obvious that she didn't want to discuss this so I didn't raise the issue.

After leaving Lena, I phoned Doctor Cohen's office. I had intended to simply ask his nurse for a referral but it was he who answered the phone.

"Margaret, how are you? It's been ages," Doctor Cohen boomed.

After I told him my concern, he insisted, "Come in now. I have a free hour."

So I did.

Chapter 64

Doctor Cohen doesn't fit the stereotype of the elderly frail. He is tall, still sturdily built, and the white streaks in his blond hair make him resemble the aging rock star which he might have been.

He has played the guitar since childhood and, after completing his medical residency, had crisscrossed America with a country-and-western band. Thankfully for his Greenwich patients, the band had never made it big. If you press him and he isn't busy, he might sing for you and very well indeed. Still, Doctor Cohen was all business with me and his first question set the tone.

"What pregnancy test did you use?" he asked.

"Something my stepmother bought in Berlin. I studied there for a term," I replied.

"Why did you test yourself? Did you miss your period?" he asked.

"No, but I was nauseous and vomiting. Gained weight and my breasts got bigger too. My stepmother advised me to," I replied.

"Hmm," Doctor Cohen mused, sitting back in his chair.

"There are two types of pregnancy tests: urine and blood. Both detect human chorionic gonadotropin, hCG, the *pregnancy hormone*. This increases rapidly after the fertilized egg implants into the uterine lining. Pregnancy tests can typically produce a positive result ten days after implantation depending on its sensitivity," he explained.

"What's the difference between the tests?" I asked.

"The blood test is more sensitive and lets the doctor monitor the pregnancy. My nurse will be back from lunch in a few minutes to draw blood. She's much better at it than me," Doctor Cohen said, with a smile.

The nurse returned, drew blood, and Doctor Cohen and I chatted while waiting for the results. He spoke of how greatly Greenwich had changed since he opened his practice. Then, it was a sleepy village, more a family town than the center of finance that it became with the influx of hedge fund wealth.

The nurse entered the room and gave Doctor Cohen a sheet of paper. He read it, frowned, and ordered, "Repeat the test."

I began worrying. My mother's fatal diagnosis had probably sounded like this.

Chapter 65

While awaiting the test's result, I only half-listened to Doctor Cohen's amusing stories. Is he trying to cheer me up before his pronouncement of doom? I asked myself.

Yes, I was in *that* mood. You've had them and know what it's like. When your depression seems more real than anything that's happening.

The nurse re-appeared a few minutes later. Doctor Cohen scanned the sheet that he had been handed and looked steadily at me.

"*What?*" I asked quickly, and jumped up.

"You're not pregnant," he said simply.

I felt stunned. How could I not be pregnant? I had gotten the positive test result in Berlin and my symptoms were *exactly* those of my two friends who had given birth. Which is what I said.

"A false positive result isn't unknown with home pregnancy tests. You may not have followed the directions exactly, or tested too early, or drank too much liquid before testing. Even at their best, they're ninety-seven percent, not one-hundred percent accurate."

"But I had the symptoms of pregnancy," I argued.

"*Sit down,*" Doctor Cohen ordered, calmly.

"A test error can also happen if the woman is taking certain drugs. You're not on any medication, are you?" he asked.

"None."

"Some illnesses can cause error but these are exceedingly rare in a teenager. I'd go for the most probable explanation which I have a feeling you won't like."

"What's that?" I asked.

"Psychology. The unconscious mind is powerful. It can cause physical symptoms that mimic virtually any medical condition. One teenager pounded his chest and insisted that he couldn't breathe. He had been in the Emergency Room five times over the previous two months but nothing medically wrong was ever found. Yet the boy insisted there *was* something wrong and he right. But it was in his life and not his body, maybe like you."

Chapter 66

"It's embarrassing. I told everyone I was pregnant," I said finally, after moments of silence.

"The mind is a wondrous thing though most people would prefer to wonder about the minds of other's. Do you want a referral to a therapist? I went when I was nearer your age," Doctor Cohen said, with a deprecating smile.

"*You*?" I asked.

"Surviving a medical residency isn't easy. It was that or smoking pot," he replied.

A laugh burst from me, both from surprise at his revelation and anxiety.

"I probably should go. I've been through a lot lately and parents don't want to hear some things," I said.

"We all need our fantasies. I do expect to treat your children but not now," Doctor Cohen said, in a reassuring tone.

I refused his offer to refer me to a shrink. My best friend, Erika, has been seeing one for nearly ten years. Her treatment is now down to one session per week. It had been two sessions per week when she considered suicide after the murder of her mother and sister. I phoned her after leaving Doctor Cohen's office.

"I'm not pregnant. I'd better see your shrink," I said tersely.

"I'll give you his number. He's very busy but tell him I sent you," Erika replied.

"Do you get points?" I asked.

It was a dumb thing to say but I was nervous, which was what I said.

"Forget it, sister," Erika replied.

We're long been like sisters. I nodded though she couldn't see it.

"How is Clarence?" I asked.

"He's adjusting to the lifestyle of a diabetic and I'm being supportive. How is your mother doing?" Erika asked.

She meant Lena. Family conversations can be confusing when they include a biological mother, an adoptive mother, and a stepmother.

"I don't know. She's not into talking about her health. Look, I can't talk now. I'm feeling too upset," I said, the words bursting from me.

"Do you want to come over?" Erika asked, with a concerned tone.

"Not now, but I will call your shrink," I promised.

Chapter 67

I called the shrink, Doctor Kandey, who was as sweet as his name implied. He was a tall, bearded man who, despite his lack of potbelly, would have resembled a mall's Santa Claus but for the small scar on his temple.

Doctor Kandey's office had the usual analyst's couch which we both ignored. Upon entering the room, he pointed toward a club chair for me to sit and sat in another club chair facing me. It didn't look like a doctor's office nor was his black pinstripe suit the usual doctor's garb.

Dr. Kandey asked me the same questions that I had been asked years earlier, during my treatment for Post-Traumatic Stress Disorder at a California military hospital. That was after my return from Tokyo where I had been held prisoner by an insane killer.

I answered the doctor's initial questions freely. I told him that I was single and a Barnard student. That, when not living at home in Greenwich, I lived in a Barnard dormitory. I said that I had no medical issues and was not taking any medication. It was only when he asked what brought me to his office that things became difficult. How much should I reveal about my life?

I decided that he didn't have to know *everything*. Like that my family consisted of *two* men who considered me their daughter, a biological mother, an adoptive mother, and a step-mother too. KISS, I told myself, using the computer programming rule that Randy spoke of: *Keep It Simple, Stupid,* and I did.

I said that Doctor Cohen's suggestion troubled me: that I wanted so strongly to be pregnant that my unconscious mind had *forced* my body to create pregnancy symptoms.

Erika told me that psychoanalysts tend to view matters in terms of years: if the patient doesn't understand a symptom *now*, then understanding it much later is just as good.

But this wouldn't work for me. I had decisions to make and needed to understand. I had to regain control over my mind, not fear that it might erupt at any moment into who knew what action. So, with the thought that Doctor Kandey was being paid four-hundred dollars a session, I leaned forward in my chair and spoke firmly.

"*Why* did my pregnancy symptoms happen?" I asked, in a tell-me-now/no-nonsense tone.

Chapter 68

Doctor Kandey leaned back in his chair and fiddled with the pen which he had been using to write notes.

"Since this is our first meeting and we haven't yet fully explored your life, I can only speak in general terms. Your unconscious mind must have had an important reason to create your pregnancy symptoms. Were you trying to become pregnant?" he asked.

"Not at all. I was shocked by the signs," I replied.

"Could there be a reason how becoming pregnant would reduce some conflict in your life?"

I didn't immediately reply. Instead, I stared at the Rorschach-like abstract painting hanging on the wall which I interpreted as a face. Then, unexpectedly, a thought occurred to me. I looked down as I felt my cheeks redden.

"*What?*" Doctor Kandey asked, softly.

"I'm embarrassed to say," I sputtered, and he waited.

"Several months before, I discovered that Randy, my boyfriend, had an affair. We were in Austin, on a trip that was to be our pre-marital honeymoon if there is such a thing."

Doctor Kandey nodded understandingly.

"I was a virgin and was sure that he was too–until I learned that he wasn't. We made up but he only expressed tenderness when I told him that I was pregnant. Could that be what I was seeking?" I asked.

"How are things going in your relationship now?"

"Fine. He seems committed and has taken my part against his parents. Separating from them has been Randy's life-long struggle."

"That explanation sounds reasonable but other stressors may have contributed. Has your recent life been so difficult that you might have hungered to relax and be taken care of?" Doctor Kandey asked.

"You might well say that," I replied, being unable to stifle a grin.

Over the previous months I had discovered my likely biological father, decided on a new career, battled criminals, and more.

Doctor Kandey just nodded, sensing that I wasn't ready to reveal more.

"We'll have to stop now. Do you want to schedule another appointment?" he asked.

"I'm not sure. Can I think about it?" I replied.

"Of course, the decision must be yours. I tell my patients that the most important thing they can gain from therapy is the conviction that they must make their own decisions, even with me. To try my suggestion but, if it doesn't work, feel free to try something else."

And, with that comment and his smile, my therapy session ended though I sensed that I might return.

Chapter 69

Though better, my mind still felt scrambled after leaving Doctor Kandey's office. It's frightening to recognize that you had lost control of yourself even if only temporarily.

"Calm down. You're just like everyone else," Erika reassured me.

I had gone directly to her home after the therapy session. Her long years of therapy made her my go-to expert on matters psychological.

"I guess you're right but it's terrifying that one's mind could produce such physical symptoms," I admitted.

"It wouldn't have had to if you had been more open to your feelings," Erika said.

"I'll try," I said somberly.

"What now?" she asked.

"Now, I'll have to tell everyone the truth and eat crow," I said.

"Not from those who love you. Stay for the group. It'll help you relax," Erika said.

The group that she referred to, *Filthy Chicks*, was created by Stephanie, a transfer student from London. When the Greenwich High School's principal refused permission to hold their meetings at the school, she called upon Erika for help. They had met at a getting-to-know-your-foreign-student association meeting that Erika had established.

Since even the influence of Erika's billionaire father couldn't change the school's decision, the group began meeting in Erika's home and this had continued.

"Despite the title, it's no different from the group that we created for our babysitters," Erika said.

When my father became disabled by Lyme disease and unable to work, Erika suggested beginning a babysitter service to earn money for me. The Greenwich Babysitter's Registry, LLC was successful and, to increase the skills of our babysitters, we held a weekly child-care educational group which quickly changed into discussions of dating and sex.

"When does the group meet?" I asked.

"Today, in a half-hour. There's just enough time for a snack," Erika said.

"But I'll be out of place there. I'm not a high school student," I objected.

"That won't matter. If you've ever had potato chips and peanut butter for dinner you'll feel right at home," Erika said.

Once again, she was right.

Chapter 70

Stephanie, the *Filthy Chick's* founder, had the posh British accent of a BBC commentator and the beatific look of a nun. Demurely dressed in an ankle-length skirt and long-sleeve blouse buttoned to her neck, her appearance would be acceptable to the most conservative religion. She also didn't wear makeup, not that her flawless skin needed it.

Stephanie was the kind of girl who, at first glance, mothers want for their sons though her opening words would shatter this illusion: "Ready to be *filthy*?" she asked us, with a malevolent grin. I later learned that this greeting opened every meeting.

Despite my initial belief, this group's topics were tamer than those of the babysitters' group that Erika and I had run. Our discussion topics had tended toward oral sex, anal sex, how early to have sex, and how much sex was too much in a relationship.

That day's concern was love and Helaine spoke first.

"I'm an addict," she said, hesitantly.

"Pot or pills?" Naomi asked.

"Neither. I seem addicted to falling in love," Helaine replied.

We leaned forward but she had a hard time starting. Love is a problem for all teenagers and I felt like a high school freshman again.

"Describe your problem like you're telling a story," Erika suggested, and Helaine began.

"I tend to fall in love too easily. When I meet a guy, I tell all my friends, 'Oh, he's cute and funny and has gorgeous blue eyes and we'd have stunning babies though I'm not sure how tall they'll be since I'm small and he's six feet three.' I sense that I'm rushing things but can't help it," Helaine said.

I wanted to say that she was being a bit psycho but Erika spoke first and more tactfully.

"You want to take it slow and not rush things. That which burns brightly can burn out fast and your attitude would terrify a boy. He's deciding what movie to see on your next date and you're totaling the cost of diapers."

The discussion became passionate and changed course.

Chapter 71

Hildegard (an old family name, she told us) provided advice: "Don't go traveling with a guy you just met."

I was shocked by this considering that she was seventeen. But she was the only child of a single parent whose job required international travel. Thus, Hildegard lived on her own much of the time and was free to make her own rules, which it was unlikely that she shared with either of her parents.

"My mom was in Dubai over Christmas so I was alone. A guy in Starbucks chatted me up and we made a date to see a movie. There was nothing good playing so I invited him home for dinner," she said.

I shared glances with Erika. The guy could have been one of those polished serial killers that we read about.

"What happened?" Erika asked.

"Nothing then. He said that he had a dinner date with friends and couldn't come but that he'd text me afterward. He never did and when I E-mailed him he said that he was going into Manhattan for the weekend to visit friends. When I checked him out on Facebook, I found that a girl in Manhattan had been writing to him so he was probably visiting her and lying to me."

"How many times did you see him?" Erika asked.

"Three times in one week and twice in a row. I thought it was going somewhere," Hildegard replied, with a downcast expression.

"You were lucky. Nothing could ever beat the guy that I met," Lucy said.

"I was returning on Amtrak from visiting my sister in Boston. Lance sat beside me and we talked. He said that his rich family was planning to open a nightclub in Stamford. He told me about a great restaurant that he had been to and show that he had seen. I gave him my number and he called the next night.

"I felt glad to go out with an older guy. My past dates were a teenage junkie, a boy who picked his nose, and another who thought that he might be gay.

"After that run of bad luck, I was so excited that I told my parents and they got so excited that my mom said to tell him 'hello' for her. But soon after we met, something seemed wrong. He told me that he was working as a manager in Macy's shoe department to get experience to manage his intended nightclub. But he paid for everything and we had a good time so I continued believing that I had lucked out.

"Our next date was a movie. When I arrived, he had a bag of McDonald's in his hand saying that he was hungry and wolfed down two burgers. During the movie, he put his feet up on the seat in front of him and farted loudly and constantly. I asked him to stop but he thought it was funny.

"Our next and last date was at a restaurant. He arrived forty minutes late and seemed drunk. He asked if I wanted to see something cool. We went to the parking lot where he pulled down his pants and showed me his purple bikini briefs."

All stared at Lucy when she finished speaking. My worries had disappeared.

Chapter 72

Contrary to my expectancy, learning that I wasn't pregnant didn't upset my parents or anyone else. They felt relieved as did I. I wasn't ready to be a mother nor was Randy prepared to be a father. We were concerned with other matters, mine being Randy's survival.

Violence didn't come naturally to him and he was entering a world where it was currency. *Must* Randy do this task? Could he still refuse to help Olga with what had become an intelligence operation?

He could have refused but didn't. Maybe because it was me who had first asked him. Maybe because he liked Olga. And possibly because he had become stirred to live an active life after meeting my uncle, Borya, the Russian general nicknamed Lucifer. This had been given him for reasons that others refused to share.

Lee's pep talks with Randy had spruced his courage. But his teenage belief of invulnerability had also returned and I viewed it my task to bring him back to reality.

"The Young boys consider you their friend but you're not. They're smart and will be a continual danger They'll tell their parents if they sense there's something wrong about you. Whatever Lee told you, there'll be no cavalry storming to your rescue. You'll be on your own," I said, trying to be brutally honest.

Randy got the message.

"I'll be careful," he said, soberly.

"The moment that you sense something isn't quite right, get out of there. Everyone has a reptilian survival instinct. Don't ignore its warning!"

Randy hugged me.

"I'll come home to you, and all in one piece," he said.

"You'd better. You've never seen me really angry. How I was in Austin was nothing," I said.

There, Randy had confessed his affair to me.

"I won't try to be a hero," Randy said, and teared up.

"You'll always be my hero," I said.

We held each other without speaking for a long time.

Chapter 73

"Randy will be OK. It's just your nerves," Erika assured me.

The dinner at the Young's apartment was scheduled for 7:00PM. Randy had planned to tell them that he needed to take the 11:10PM return train to Greenwich. We eagerly awaited him at Grand Central Station's downstairs level.

Reminding myself of Randy's fictional situation didn't calm me. That, for the Young's, he was simply a naïve college student. A youth to help their children with their Raspberry Pi projects and make small talk during dinner. What could go wrong? I asked myself, before replying aloud, "Everything."

"Huh?" Erika asked.

She was picking up this maddening verbal response from me.

"It's wracking my nerves. If things go down, I don't trust Randy's ability to defend himself. He's too much a thinker, too deliberate and not spontaneous enough," I said.

"He's had training," Erika responded.

"But not nearly enough. I wish that I was with him. I'd kill any bastard that even mussed his hair," I said.

"That's love," Erika said, after staring at me for a moment.

Randy arrived late and we had to run to catch the train. I had earlier bought bottles of water and packets of nuts at the newsstand and we snacked while talking.

We occupied a four-seater at the end of the last car and spoke so softly that no passenger could overhear us. I didn't have to ask what happened. Randy was bursting to tell us.

"We had a typical American meal: meat loaf and mashed. String beans too though I don't particularly like them," Randy said.

Randy was "high" from relief and being playful. At another time, I would have smiled at his teasing but not then. Silence can communicate more than words. I remained silent and stared at him.

"OK," he said quickly, and briefly described what had happened.

Chapter 74

"Mostly nothing happened," Randy said.

"OK, but describe *nothing* exactly as it happened," I said.

"I arrived at the apartment house ten minutes early. The doorman opened the door and the man at the lobby desk called upstairs to announce me. I rode the elevator to the ninth floor.

"I didn't have to ring the bell since the boys were standing by the open door. They smiled and I smiled back and entered the apartment. There, their parents were waiting. They introduced themselves and the boys took me to their room.

"They had the latest, third generation Raspberry Pi model. It has a 1.2 Gh, quad-core, 64-bit CPU, 802.11n wireless, Bluetooth 4.1, and 1GB RAM. They wanted to build a computer.

"I had brought an old ThinkPad with me. Also, a USB stick on which I'd burned the Raspberry PI's PIXEL desktop program to show them what their finished product would look like. I said that I'd have to modify the software to make it installable. This gave me a reason to return," Randy said.

"Did their parents watch while you were with them?" Erica asked.

"For a while but they soon got bored. Every few minutes they'd drop in and ask if we wanted a snack but that was all," Randy replied.

"Did you plant the audio-video receiver?" I asked.

"Not yet, give me time. Would it help to get the family to London?" Randy asked.

"Huh?" I ejaculated quickly, before catching myself.

"There's a a huge EdTech event in London next month with workshops spread over four days. If it would help, I might be able to persuade them to go."

Anxiety flooded through me for I didn't like this suggestion. Randy would be unprotected in London–and beset by fascinating English girls too! I didn't yet fully trust him. His recent infidelity had left its mark.

"Raise this possibility with Lee, whether he feels it would be helpful. Being outside American authority could present complications," I said.

"OK," Randy agreed.

"Did anything else happen?" I asked.

"Not really except for a visitor. He arrived during dinner and was quickly shuttled from the room."

"Was there anything particular about him?" Erika asked.

"Just that he limped, wore thick-lensed glasses, and stared at me. One more thing. Lee has given me a code name: *Hermes*."

"Why that?" I asked.

"Probably because in Greek mythology, Zeus was king of the Gods and his son, Hermes, was their messenger," Erika explained.

I didn't like what was happening. Randy was getting into something bigger and more dangerous, out of anyone's control. But my saying this would just increase his anxiety and thus his risk.

So instead, I leaned over and kissed him and he smiled confidently.

Chapter 75

Lee awaited us at Erika's home which had become our command center. Her father, Hamilton ("call me Harry"), had necessarily been brought into the operation. His bodyguards wouldn't tolerate strangers in the house nor would Harry's business guests appreciate them. Thus, we all slipped in-and-out inconspicuously.

Erika's large bedroom was an unusual place for such meetings but it was also the safest. No one, not even her father, dared intrude, and with drinks and snacks from the kitchen it was as good as any place.

Present on the following Sunday morning were Lee, his technical assistant, Bill, his office assistant, Leona, Erika, Olga, me, and Randy. He described his experience at the Young's apartment and Lee had him repeat it twice before asking questions.

"The man with the limp. Could you recognize him from photos?" Lee asked.

"I'd try," Randy replied.

"How did the parents behave with each other. Who seemed the boss?" Lee asked.

"I'm not sure since there was just small talk. But he glanced at her several times, as if for approval before speaking so it could be her," Randy replied.

"That was a good observation. You're talented," Lee said, approvingly.

Randy blushed and looked down. He doesn't accept compliments well.

"How soon can you install the audio-visual transmitter?" Bill asked.

"How soon can you get me the case for the Raspberry PI?" Randy replied.

Bill drew from his briefcase a small metal box that Randy inspected closely.

"I'll fix the device into it tonight and leave it at the apartment during my next visit," Randy said.

"When is that?" Bill asked.

"Next Friday, after the boys let out from school. It's a good time. There'll be only me, the boys, and the au pair in the apartment.

Everybody but me looked pleased. I thought of how gorgeous the au pair was.

Chapter 76

I was worn out when the meeting ended but Randy's success had lowered the tension in the room. Lee and his colleagues gathered their stuff and left and the rest of us went to our bedrooms. Erika's forty-million-dollar home is never short of accommodations and toiletry supplies. Except for lacking room service, it resembles a well-run hotel.

Randy grabbed for me as soon as we were alone but I pushed him off. We needed to talk.

"What have you found about my brother?" I asked, with an annoyed tone.

He had said nothing about him since finding the computer link between the adoption of my brother and that of Olga's sons. The government's interest in the Young boys had pushed my brother's existence from all minds except mine.

"I'll get onto it, I promise," Randy said, apologetically.

I nodded and removed my hand from his. He likes undressing me and I don't object.

Later, he left the bed and got out his laptop.

I covered myself with the bedsheet and sat up.

"What?" I asked.

"An idea just hit me about your brother's file. God, I've been an idiot," Randy said.

Randy doesn't like being interrupted when he's working so I fell back onto the bed, feeling more relaxed. Sex has that effect.

Margaret in Manhattan

"I was thinking that the files must contain a means of locating the adoptees, that a bit of code might be it and it was. It's a simple letter switch, hidden within the log-in page photos."

"Take this down," Randy said absent-mindedly, a few minutes later.

I carefully wrote the letters as Randy spoke them.

"They make no sense," I said, handing the sheet of paper to him.

He concentrated on the letters, rearranging them in his mind.

"Not as they're written but if the letters are moved one place up the alphabet they do," Randy said.

I looked how he had rearranged the letters and he was right.

Chapter 77

"I've been so stupid. They were using the equivalent of Prattle and it worked. God, but I'm dumb," Randy said.

Despite his success, he looked dejected and I had no idea why. Are his unreasoned mood swings something that I need confront during our future married life? I sked myself

"Randy, your Yale computer professor called you 'a genius.' I don't doubt this nor should you. You've apparently succeeded so what's bothering you?" I asked, trying to sound both sympathetic and irritated.

Randy pulled himself together. We were a source of strength to each other.

"I'm sorry. I get like this when I finally grasp something that I should have realized or think I should have. The Prattle type system threw me though it shouldn't have since me and my professor helped develop it. Which just shows you what good software it is," Randy said, with a smile that I welcomed.

I asked the expected question, partly because explaining technical matters relaxes Randy and because it might be something that I should know.

"What is *Prattle*?"

"Do you know what cyber-warfare is?" Randy answered, adopting a professorial tone.

Though his elementary question was a put-down, I knew he didn't mean it. It was simply the way he taught. I nodded.

"Good. Well, when using the Internet, one is continually at war. Enemies are trying to destroy your network and learn your secrets. So, to reduce their ability, I thought of using a bit of trickery. Like when we get our parents to agree with what we want without pressuring them," Randy said.

"That's clever," I said.

"That's what my professor thought too and why the Air Force Research Lab funded our work. With most of the money going to Yale of course," Randy said.

He smiled understandingly, having already learned the ways of academic research.

"Prattle creates data that misleads an attacker who has penetrated a network. This makes them doubt what they have learned or causes them to make mistakes which increases their likelihood of being detected.

"The program generates data that is nearly identical to ordinary traffic but includes slight changes to meet the organization's goals. Adding *false signal*, we call it."

When Randy paused to take a breath, I spoke my interpretation of his explanation.

"You want to make them easier to detect by watermarking data to tie them to a location for identification, and to subtly change details of valuable information to confuse or misdirect the enemy," I summarized.

After a momentary silence, Randy spoke.

"I'm always underestimating you, aren't I?" he asked.

As reply, I pulled him back onto the bed.

Chapter 78

Randy thought that he had found my brother, Blake, giving this a probability of seventy-five percent.

"Where is he?" I asked.

"You won't believe it!" Randy replied, teasingly.

"Randy!" I said, warningly.

"A few miles from the Young's apartment, on Manhattan's West Side," he replied.

"You have an address?" I asked, hesitantly.

I couldn't quite believe it. Months before, my learning that I had a twin brother was a shock. I wasn't yet prepared for the possibility of meeting him.

"I don't know," I mused aloud.

"What?"

"About meeting Blake."

"He's no longer Blake. His name is now Creighton," Randy said.

My eyes became vacant and I felt faint. Randy put his arm around me and held me tight.

"It's too much all at once. First, Lena's illness, then learning that I had a long-lost twin brother who might have been groomed as a spy, and finally that I wasn't pregnant as I had believed. It's all too much," I said, and began crying.

"It's all right, baby," Randy said, as I clung to him.

"Maybe I should see that therapist again," I said.

"Possibly, but you might want to be careful what you tell him. Blake, or Creighton, could be involved in illegal activity. I wouldn't reveal this or what we've been doing. If you want to keep a secret, you don't talk about it," Randy said.

This was originally my line so I couldn't help but agree.

"I could raise the issue indirectly. How should one relate to a sibling that they've never known? There must be other cases. Besides, what I'm dealing with is stress and that's his job," I said.

"Mine too, you'll always have me," Randy said.

"I'll always have you," I repeated.

At that moment, I felt sure that we would share a long life together.

Chapter 79

Randy told Lee what he had discovered about my brother. I had first opposed this but finally agreed that we had no choice. In the scheme of national interests, family matters don't count. Moreover, considering that Creighton was still a teenager, we might gain friendly influence to help him.

"However it turns out, it'll be a mess," Randy said, and I agreed.

The only change in the government activity was that surveillance was placed on Creighton's family so they couldn't again disappear.

Randy's meetings with the boys continued. He had helped them build two micro-computers, one for each.

"We need more audio-visual coverage, in the living room and the parents' room," Lee ordered.

Randy hoped to accomplish this with Raspberry PI presents that he and the boys would create: an alarm clock to hold digital photos, and a bird cage containing an electronic bird which sang according to a schedule.

Randy joked that its song would be *The Star-Spangled Banner* and this produced smiles. The gadget was so cute that I asked him to build one for my baby sister.

"Once this is over," he promised.

Meanwhile, life went on. College classes began in a month and we hadn't yet decided whether to return to Berlin or remain in America. This decision was easier when I believed myself to be pregnant. Then, a woman wants to be close to her mother.

I returned to Doctor Kandey's office. Erika said that therapy creates dependency and this bothered me, even if it related only to working on my emotional problems. But I'll give it another shot, I told her.

Once again, I ignored Doctor Kandey's inviting couch and sat on the club chair opposite him. He apologized for the chill in the office.

"I just arrived and turned on the electric heater. The insurance company next door controls the building's heating. Their secretary is always hot so she turns it off an hour after she arrives. We've squabbled about it for years," he said.

"What brings you back?" he asked, after a minute of silence.

I shrugged, feeling unable to speak. Tears strangled my words when I finally did.

"You're suffering," Doctor Kandey said, softly.

"You don't know the half of it," I said, as I dried my eyes.

Chapter 80

The office felt frozen with silence. Revealing one's life is no simple manner. Everyone has secrets, those which merely embarrass and those which shouldn't be told. And the only sure way to keep a secret is not to tell it.

But it was the stress from secrets which had driven me crazy and created the false symptoms that I was pregnant. Could I touch on these matters without revealing their details? I asked myself, and then tried.

"I haven't told you some things," I began.

"It takes time to trust someone," Doctor Kandey said, sympathetically.

"I've led a complicated life. I was adopted at birth and only recently learned the identity of my mother and biological father. I'm not even sure of that since two men consider me their child. My mother had concurrent affairs with both."

"That *is* a story," Doctor Kandey replied in an even tone.

"It's not as bad as it sounds since they know and respect each other and I love them all. They aren't ordinary people. My adoptive father is a respected lawyer. My father in London, Peter, is a former British spy and Vladimir, my father in Berlin, is a former Russian general who now runs a security company."

"That certainly is some story," Doctor Kandey said.

"It gets better, or worse. I've narrowly avoiding death while helping others," I said.

"Would you feel comfortable describing these events?" Doctor Kandey asked.

"I would, but can't. Governments were involved and they were never made public," I replied.

"I understand. Before moving to Greenwich, I practiced in Washington and several of my patients were CIA employees. I had to get a security clearance to treat them and still hold it. How do you see me as helping you?" he asked.

I involuntarily choked up and began crying. I must be going crazy, I told myself, and began speaking even before the tears stopped flowing.

"I recently learned that I have a twin brother. I'll need your help to save him," I said.

Chapter 81

"What's your brother's situation?" Doctor Kandey asked.

I hesitated though having expected this logical question. My dilemma remained: how much should I reveal? Well, in for a penny, in for a pound, I told myself, using this ancient English proverb.

"Have you seen the TV series, *The Americans*?" I asked.

"No. I'm into old movies: Hitchcock, Bergmann, those."

"You might like it. It's a popular show about an apparently American family who are Russian sleeper agents, spies that were planted to do mischief. It's not realistic as these things go. Real spies would flee America after just one of their troubles," I said.

"You sound like an expert," Doctor Kandey said, with a small smile.

"I've had a good teacher: a father who was a celebrated spy," I replied.

Doctor Kandey smiled again.

"What are you saying?" he asked.

"I'm saying that my brother, Creighton, was illegally adopted by a couple who are probable sleeper agents. He may already have been brainwashed to do their bidding," I answered.

"How are you involved?" Doctor Kandey asked.

"My boyfriend, Randy, is a computer genius. He located him for me."

"So there are basically two reasons why you're here. The first is to better cope with your stress, and the second is to advise you how to relate with your brother when you meet. It'll be a shock for both of you even apart from any actions of the Justice Department."

"You couldn't have said it better," I said.

I leaned back and awaited his answers.

Chapter 82

"You're afraid that your symptoms will return out-of-the-blue and paralyze you," Doctor Kandey said.

I nodded.

"OK, but before explaining this, may I offer some advice for Randy?" Doctor Kandcy asked.

I again nodded though feeling puzzled.

"He's involved in something that is beyond his pay grade, to put it mildly. Whatever the government asks him to do, tell him not to refuse. He should say 'I'll think about it,' or 'That's interesting,' but he must not refuse!"

"Why not?" I asked.

"I've known people like those he's working for. The only ones who count are themselves. If you're not with them then you're a risk to be eliminated along with anyone else who knows what's going on. You could be in danger too."

"They'd never harm me! They must have checked me out and know my background. Vladimir's security firm is really a private army. Family is important to Russians. He'd have anyone who harmed me killed and Peter might do the same," I said.

"You have uncommon relatives," Doctor Kandey said, with another of his small smiles.

I returned his smile though feeling shaken. Being murdered by a fellow American wasn't a possibility that I had considered.

Doctor Kandey sensed my distress.

"I felt that I had to say it," he said, a bit apologetically, closing that topic.

"Now, back to your stress. What you've experienced is normal. The mind has a limited capacity to tolerate stress and you exceeded it. It reacted by creating the symptoms of false pregnancy, to frighten you into seeking help and why you're now here.

"You developed what doctors describe as a *psychosomatic disorder*. People like to think that we can make ourselves well. 'Having a positive attitude is important,' many say, and it's true. But people can also do the opposite: they can *think themselves sick*.

"Though causing real pain and disability, psychosomatic disorders are unlike other illnesses for they obey no rules. They can affect any part of the body and even many parts simultaneously. In extreme cases, they can cause paralysis or convulsions or blindness.

"Almost any symptom imaginable can become real when we are upset. Many people who consult their doctor have no medical cause for their distress because there is none. Their symptoms reflect emotional pain, as happened with you.

"But symptoms are also logical. They happen for a reason and aren't created without it. When words are unavailable, our bodies speak and we must listen.

"Your current activity is highly stressful but I feel that it was the personal issues that dominated. You sound well experienced with the other involvements and can probably do them with your eyes closed," Doctor Kandey said.

"It wouldn't be advisable," I said, with a smile.

"No, probably not," he said, again adding his own brief smile.

Chapter 83

"Now, about your long-lost brother," Doctor Kandey said.

"How can I possibly relate to him or he to me? I'll be turning his world upside down," I said, leaning forward in my chair.

"Creighton might consider your arrival a blessing. That his mother and sister so loved him that they searched for him, wherever he was and whatever he was doing," Doctor Kandey replied.

"I hadn't thought of that."

"Experiencing a life like the TV show, *The Americans*, is unique but there are similar cases. One teenager was kidnapped at birth and only eighteen years later did she learn who her real parents were. After the kidnapper's arrest, the girl said that she believed the abductor to have loved her completely.

"It took time for the girl to make sense of her life since it was basically erased. She was forced to question everything that she had been told and had believed to be true.

"There have been other such cases. Another teenager didn't realize that she had been kidnapped until seeing her picture on a milk carton.

"But Creighton might also be very angry at his biological mother, feeling that she should have tried harder to find him. This, even though in their dreams it's the parent who raised them that they love. He might develop problems with intimacy, with trusting other people," Doctor Kandey concluded.

"What should I tell him when we meet?" I asked.

"Tell him the truth: that you are his sister and have come to bring him home. After that, you'll have to see what happens."

"Like so much in life," I said.

"Approach him with confidence. The best things in life aren't predicted," Doctor Kandey said.

I murmured to myself as I stood.

"*What*?" he asked.

"Love comes in many different shapes and sizes," I said.

"You've learned a profound lesson at so young an age," Doctor Kandey said.

Chapter 84

I felt calmer immediately after leaving Doctor Kandey's office but didn't stay that way. Others noticed, even my youngest sister, Claudine.

"You're worried," she said, as we washed breakfast dishes on the following morning.

Now, again living at home as a (not-pregnant) dutiful daughter, I had been drafted into doing family chores.

"Just a bit. Older people have more worries," I lied.

Claudine stared at me for a long moment but didn't say anything. Her painful past had made her more perceptive than most grade schoolers.

The next hour, while distractedly scanning the upcoming Barnard College course bulletin, I began thinking seriously. There are times when one needs help and it is a mistake not to seek it.

What Doctor Kandey said about Lee frightened me. If necessary, I could disappear in Berlin but Randy wasn't that kind of person. Despite his Navy SEAL fantasies of heroism, he would always be a thinker not a doer, and red meat for the likes of Lee. We needed help and, when a teenager needs help, they must turn to their parents. Phone Vladimir, I ordered myself, and did.

After small talk about my toddler step-sister and pregnant step-mother, Vladimir stopped me, using Claudine's identical phrase.

"You're worried. What's wrong?" he asked.

"You have a son!" I said abruptly.

181

"I have two sons."

"You now have three. Lena told me that I have a twin brother and I'm searching for him," I said.

Vladimir is usually quick to respond but this news threw him.

"You have a twin brother," he mused, and murmured something in Russian.

"*What?*" I asked.

'A proverb about the blessings of old age. Tell me about him," he ordered, and I did.

Vladimir knew of Olga's search for her stolen twins but not of their connection with Creighton or their grooming as sleeper agents.

"You are treading on dangerous paths," he said.

"Don't I know it," I said, and told him of Doctor Kandey's observation.

"He is a wise doctor. Keep seeing him," Vladimir ordered.

"I plan to," I replied.

"I'll call our contact in Washington and inform Borya. He will educate Lee."

"Thank you, papa," I said.

My worry was gone when we hung up. Borya, my uncle, was a formidable Russian general. Now, for the first time, I considered his nickname with thankfulness and not dread. It is *Lucifer*, the Devil.

Chapter 85

I felt better the next morning and others noticed.

"You had looked so depressed but now seem your usual self," my mother said.

I *was* better. Gaining Vladimir's help had lifted my spirits and I no longer felt tormented by my predicament. He had taken it onto his shoulders and I could resume my normal life.

I hadn't told Randy what Doctor Kandey said. Randy is the nervous type and it would have terrified him. Though we weren't married, I had long before adopted wifely duties. These included suffering his worries and bolstering his delicate self-esteem. Telling him proved unnecessary for Lee pulled me aside at our next meeting.

"I've gotten phone calls about you and Randy," he said.

"Oh?" I replied, in an innocent tone.

"One was from a Russian general who said that he was your uncle," Lee said.

"That's true. My father in Berlin is a retired Russian general too," I said.

"They were interesting conversations," Lee said.

He then turned back to the others. He had told me, subtly, that he took seriously Borya's threat: things would not go well for him if Randy or I were harmed. Whatever dangers occurred, they wouldn't arise from his camp.

But parents worry and Peter, my English father, phoned me that evening.

"Vladimir told me what's going on. Do you need me there?" he asked.

"No, but thanks much. Lee got the message," I said.

"OK, but more will be needed to protect my son," Peter said.

As I explained, my family is complicated: both me and my brother might be Peter's or Vladimir's children. A DNA test was never performed and it was now too late for all concerned.

"I do miss you and grandma," I said,

I had last visited them in London over the previous summer.

"We've missed you too. What would you say to our visit? Your brother's situation will require negotiation in Washington and grandma would love to catch-up," Peter said.

What was not to like?

Chapter 86

What was not to like was feeling confused. In addition to my adoptive father, I had two other fathers, both of whom now considered yet another child to be their own. It was inevitable that, one day, all would meet and I feared the resultant collision. Creighton might well be Peter's child, which wasn't what I had told Vladimir. My earlier calm was gone.

"Tell Doctor Kandey about it," Erika advised me, when I described the situation to her.

When I did, his initial comment matched mine: "Wow!"

"I have two questions. First, can twins have different fathers and be identical rather than fraternal twins? The second is what will likely be Peter's and Vladimir's reactions upon learning the truth. Either could be my parent or Creighton's parent or have parented both of us," I said.

Doctor Kandey leaned back in his chair.

"Your first question is pure biology and easiest to answer. It's unlikely that you are identical twins since they're usually of the same gender, two boys or two girls. Rarely, identical twins will form from an egg and sperm that begin as males, sharing XY chromosomes, and then change to become a male and a female.

"It happens when one-half of the split fertilized egg loses a copy of its genetically encoded Y chromosome. This female will lack the hormones needed for proper growth and to reproduce resulting in *Turner Syndrome.* But this rare condition affects very few twins. Since you're normal, it doesn't concern you.

"Nonidentical, or fraternal, twins occur when a woman produced two separate eggs which are then fertilized by different sperm cells. The resulting twins can look alike but have separate genetic identities. They're like children of the same parents who are born during different pregnancies.

"These twins form when two eggs are released during the same ovulation. Sometimes the eggs release simultaneously. At other times the ovaries first release one egg which, after fertilization, begins moving to the uterus to attach.

"The ovaries then release a second egg which is fertilized by a later act of sexual intercourse, possibly with two separate fathers. Here, the children are genetically half-siblings born from separate pregnancies. This *superfecundation* isn't rare. One to two percent of fraternal twins have different fathers. I once testified in a paternal lawsuit involving this."

"You're saying that Creighton could be either my half-brother or my full-brother," I said.

"Exactly," Doctor Kandey said, before continuing.

Chapter 87

"To answer your question about Peter's and Vladimir's probable reactions to learning the truth: I don't know. You'll have to see what happens. The situation is easier since both Vladimir and Peter know you grew up with adoptive parents. Creighton had the same situation and that's something you share. But I don't expect it to go badly.

"Vladimir and Peter are sophisticated. Since Peter has no children and Vladimir does, it might be harder on Peter if the child turns out not to be his but I expect that he'll deal with it. Since it's unlikely that DNA tests will be done, you'll have to rely on who Creighton resembles. You would be amazed at how parents judge this."

"So, there's not much for me to do," I said.

"No more than being the most supportive sister to Creighton that you can," Doctor Kandey said.

"That's understood," I murmured.

"He'll face hard times if the case arouses publicity. Referring him for therapy would be helpful," Doctor Kandey said.

I had been thinking that too.

"Would you treat him?" I asked.

Doctor Kandey shook his head.

"That wouldn't be wise. To treat relatives or friends simultaneously, the doctor must be able to psychologically separate them. I'm already treating you and Claudine and Erika. Another member of your circle would be too much for me but I could refer you to another doctor," Doctor Kandey suggested.

"OK. It's not yet known where Creighton will live. That depends on how the negotiations in Washington turn out, if he'll be charged as an enemy agent," I said.

"Creighton has led a complicated life," Doctor Kandey said.

This was such an understatement that I could only nod.

Chapter 88

Often when something seems settled it turns out that it isn't. While Randy's meetings with the Young children continued as usual, something appeared to be happening with Creighton's family. They had *twice* eluded surveillance. Did this reflect their excellent spy tradecraft or their watchers' errors? No one was sure.

Though Creighton was my brother, Randy and I had been cut out of this operation. When I asked Lee how things were developing, his answer was an uninformative "fine." I learned the facts from Peter.

From his perspective, things were *not* going fine. The discussions in Washington were going badly. There, sleeper agents were considered as nasty as snipers and a quick death was wished on both.

But in courtroom, not battlefield America, the death penalty wasn't possible. Depending on which nation the sleeper agents owed allegiance to, they might be swapped for imprisoned Americans.

This possibility, though better than living in a Supermax prison, would provide little comfort for me or Vladimir or Peter and certainly not Creighton. No one chooses their parents. If this were possible, many would prefer a different family.

While we waited and worried, my English grandmother, Victoria, settled into Erika's home, mine being too small. As a debutante, Victoria had been presented to the Queen and a folding cot wouldn't do.

Victoria and Peter had stayed at Erika's home once before when they surprised me with a Welcome Home party upon my return from London.

Victoria, like her nineteenth century royal namesake, has a regal presence. She had tutored me on courteous behavior while in London and Erika's father hoped the same for his daughter. But our first dinner conversation centered on Peter.

"How did Peter happen to become a spy?" I asked.

Chapter 89

Though it is unusual to call a parent by their first name, I do this with Peter. We first met when I was a teenager and this seemed natural. Having had adoptive parents since birth, addressing him otherwise would have felt odd. He hadn't objected and neither had Victoria who I also address by her first name.

Randy was mopey at the dinner but his interest was aroused by my question. Still, I hoped that further spying would not be in his future.

"I'm not sure how much was accidental and how much was planned," Victoria began.

"Peter was obsessed with codes since childhood and having a military career runs in the family. He studied languages at University and earned a First. At graduation, a lecturer asked if he wanted to 'do something stimulating' in the foreign service.

"Despite modern recruitment methods, the trusted old-boy network is still favored by Britain's Secret Intelligence Service. Key universities have lecturers on the lookout for suitable recruits."

Clarence, Erika's fiancée, looked intently at Victoria as she spoke. Despite being a computer genius, I began fearing for his future too.

"Peter was invited to chat over tea at the Carlton House which overlooks St. James Park, and to lunch a week later. Then followed an absurd mini-exam: 'Place the following in order of social precedence: earl, duke, baron, marquis."

Clarence interrupted Victoria with the correct answer.

"Excellent. Perhaps you should contact your CIA," she said, with a smile.

"I have dual Canadian-American citizenship," Clarence said, returning her smile.

"Then you might want to speak with Peter about joining the Secret Intelligence Service," Victoria said.

I shared a disapproving glance with Erika as Victoria continued.

"That's all I know apart from Peter's publicized adventures. For more, you'll have to ask him."

Almost as if on cue, Peter entered the room. Looking haggard, he kissed his mother distractedly before sitting down.

Chapter 90

Peter is much the typical reserved Englishman who speaks calmly no matter what disaster is happening. Having a stiff upper lip, people call it. So, apart from those who knew him well, the others didn't seem to notice his upset.

After he sat next to me, I asked him softly, "What's wrong?"

"After dinner," he murmured, with a smile that wasn't quite real.

After dinner was longer than I could hardly bear.

Erika's cook, maybe in recognition of Victoria's regal presence, outdid herself. Thankfully, I could discourage her from the dishes that she was considering: Stargazy Pie, Black Pudding with Liquor, and Mushy Peas.

I ate English food during my summer in London and wasn't hungry to repeat it, to make one of my bad puns.

Stargazy pie is baked pilchards, eggs, and potatoes with a pastry top. It's named for the way that the fish poke their heads from the crust. To this the cook had thought of adding Liquor, a sauce of parsley and vinegar.

Black Pudding is blood sausage, and Mushy Peas are marrowfat peas (peas that mature in the field) that are soaked overnight and then boiled with sugar and salt to form a green mush.

Compared with these, the English breakfast of baked beans on toast is a delight.

I suggested to the cook that, since the meal was a celebration, it could resemble an English Christmas dinner.

She readily agreed, possibly already doubting her initial choices.

What we wound up with differed little from most American Christmas dinners: caviar on crackers, baked salmon, roast turkey, side dishes of Brussels sprouts with chestnuts and sage, carrots, red cabbage, and roast potatoes. The bacon/sausage/prune rolls were an English addition.

For dessert we had plum pudding, and Cherry Trifle which is layers of custard, cream, jelly, and sponge cake. Very sweet and biologically targeted for your hips.

Conversation during the meal was small talk. Erika spoke of Greenwich events and Victoria spoke of London happenings. My baby sister, Claudine, stopped conversation with her loud question of whether girls *must* shave their legs. My mother's coughing fit followed.

To move things along, I praised and made an exaggerated show of passing around the plum pudding as Claudine adopted an innocent pose. She knew exactly what she had done and so did the rest of us. The adult conversation bored her and she had shown this.

After dinner, the children went to the basement's elaborate play room while the adults settled in the spacious living room. I steered Peter to a corner. He held a glass of Scotch and I had cranberry juice.

"What's wrong?" I asked, in a low voice.

Chapter 91

"*What's wrong* was my discussion with your government's officials. I promised them the sun, moon, and stars: that our company would do what we ordinarily wouldn't. They won't budge about prosecuting Creighton." Peter said.

During the silence that followed, I peered into my cranberry juice as if inspiration lay there.

"But he's nineteen and didn't choose his parents!" I insisted.

"That was my point too though their attitude may be unimportant since his family has fled," Peter said.

"I hadn't heard," I said.

"The Agency is embarrassed. It's not something they're advertising to a new administration that wants to make changes and cut budgets," Peter said.

"We can't leave him hanging. We must find him," I said.

"I agree, and agents are checking the surveillance tapes. Randy is a computer genius. Maybe he can find something they've missed," Peter said.

With that, he retrieved a USB flash drive from his vest pocket and handed it to me.

"Their files, from our friends in the new administration," he said simply.

While silently watching the others in the room, an idea occurred to me.

"Can you get me the names and phone numbers of senior Justice Department officials?" I asked.

"I wouldn't advise calling them," Peter replied.

"That's not what I was thinking. It would be useful to gain leverage," I said.

Peter stared at me thoughtfully.

"I have a feeling that your idea isn't something I want to hear," he said.

"Nothing may come of it," I said.

"Would the company's American contracts be threatened if your action became public?" Peter asked.

"There's that too," I admitted, smiling sweetly.

"Why am I not surprised?" Peter asked.

It wasn't a real question so I answered it with mine.

"Because I'm your daughter?"

Then wasn't the moment to discuss my uncertain ancestry.

Chapter 92

"I'll get the names for you," Peter said, adding the advice that I had often been given: "Don't get caught!"

My plan was as old as mankind: to blackmail the person who possessed authority to make decisions about Creighton. To accomplish this, I needed embarrassing information about their life. It could be anything: finding the mistress of a married man; discovering drug addiction or financial impropriety. Any fact that they would not want publicized and could destroy their comfortable life.

Who were these officials and what their weaknesses? Gaining this information required help.

Being strong means knowing when to seek help, my lawyer-father often says, and that's what I did. While driving Randy home, I summarized the points of my idea clearly.

"Nowadays, people's lives are lived on their phones. I want you to intercept their calls and gain compromising information. We need this to bargain for Creighton's freedom—which he deserves!" I said.

"I agree but we could lose our freedom along the way. Do you realize how many laws we'd be breaking?" Randy asked.

"Then we'd better not get caught," I replied.

"We'd better not but those computer skills aren't my expertise and you need high-level skill to avoid being caught," he said, with a sigh.

I squeezed his thigh.

Margaret in Manhattan

"I have a friend who can do it but you won't like him," Randy added, with a smile.

Chapter 93

I might have said that I hadn't met *any* of his friends who weren't originally mine. Like many scientists, Randy is a loner but saying this would be hurtful.

"I liked all your friends," I said.

"Well, Lincoln is...*different*. He's unique," Randy said.

"We're all unique," I said.

"Yes, but..."

"Spit it out."

"He rarely showers and his clothes look like they came from a dumpster. I'm his only friend and he's never had a girlfriend. He avoids classes and survives Yale only because he's brilliant," Randy said.

"So are you," I said.

"No, I'm smart but he's *brilliant*," Randy insisted.

Playing word games isn't my style so I didn't argue. What was important was if his friend could do what we needed, not whether to invite him to a party. Which is what I said.

"Oh, he can hack into any system. The NSA salivates at the thought of hiring him but it's hard even to get him to leave his room," Randy said.

"He needs a girlfriend," I said.

"Aiding that would be saintly deed," Randy said, with a small smile.

"If that's what it takes to save Creighton, I'll do it," I said.

"Be his friend but no more than that," Randy said, in a warning tone.

"That wasn't my idea even if he showers daily," I replied.

My first thought, upon seeing Lincoln, was wondering if he was named after his presidential namesake since both were tall and gaunt. But there their resemblance ended. Our Lincoln had a red ponytail and wore clothes that caused me to wonder if he were colorblind.

Surprisingly, his mustache was carefully trimmed and with edges so sharp that I wondered if it was waxed. His odor, whether bodily or from unwashed clothes, was noticeable. I smiled, and extended my hand when we met.

"Randy says you're a genius," I said.

When Lincoln blushed at receiving a compliment as Randy always does, I sensed their similarity and why they were friends.

Chapter 94

Ignoring Lincoln's body odor was hard but I tried. I told myself that it had nothing to do with the kind of person he is though knowing this was incorrect. Having a noticeable body odor indicates that a person is ill in their mind or body. Considering Lincoln's youth and what Randy had shared, I sensed it was his mind that was troubled.

But I also didn't doubt that he was smart. Like Randy, he could explain technical matters in an orderly, understandable fashion.

"We worked on Prattle together," Randy said, by way of introduction.

Then, with the thought that I might have forgotten what Prattle was, he added, "the Air Force Lab's cyber-deception system."

"It's a lovely day. Let's sit outside," I suggested.

This was for the obvious reason but Lincoln didn't appear to take offense. Randy had said that Lincoln didn't like leaving his comfort zone so we met him on the Yale campus where outdoor benches are plentiful. It was between school terms and few students were around. With privacy assured, I told Lincoln what was needed.

"I'm trying to locate my twin brother. He was illegally adopted at birth by a low-life couple. The police aren't helping so we're all he has. Our mother is dying and she wants us together before it's too late," I said.

This explanation wasn't wholly true but it told enough and pulled at the heartstrings. I remained silent for a few moments to let my story sink in.

"Locating him will require illegal wiretapping. Will you help us?" I asked, looking directly into Lincoln's eyes.

I didn't bat my eyes but my cracked voice said it all.

"Of course. Randy is my friend," he said.

I reached over and squeezed his hand. Surprisingly, it was clean and chapped from extreme scrubbing. Lincoln is more puzzling than I thought, I told myself.

He sat up straight with a professorial posture.

"Let me explain what you want," he said, in a firm, assured voice.

Chapter 95

"There are two types of telephones: common, and crypto or TopSec. Cryptophones protect calls from interception using algorithms to scramble communication.

"Common phones are used by most people. These have minimal protection since data is encrypted only between the phone and the base station, not over the fixed networks. Government intelligence agencies suck in calls like a giant vacuum cleaner. Am I clear so far?" Lincoln asked.

"Crystal," I said, with a smile.

His return smile transformed his face from the scowl that it had held since we met.

"Cryptophones provide reasonable but not absolute security. They contain a crypto chip with two algorithms, 256-bit keys using AES and Twofish as counter mode stream ciphers. Using these together means that a far stronger encryption is achieved than with only one algorithm. If a weakness is discovered in one of the algorithms the second ensures a margin of security.

"This *fall back* system uses very long keys, a 4096-bit Diffie-Hellman shared secret exchange. It hashes the resulting 4096 bits to the 256-bit session key by means of SHA256, resulting in a product that provides the highest possible security achievable today.

"But even with these precautions, security can never be absolute. So to prevent a man-in-the-middle attack, a six-letter hash is generated from the Diffie-Hellman result and displayed to the user. They then read three letters over the encrypted line to their communication partner who verifies the three letters that were read. If there is a difference in the six letters, a man-in-the-middle attack has been detected."

My eyes had begun to glaze when Randy interrupted.

"Margaret doesn't need to know all that. Just that you can do what is needed," he said.

"Does a dog have fleas?" Lincoln asked.

Chapter 96

I handed the USB thumb drive which Peter had given me to Lincoln.

"These are the only files that we have. We need the families' locations and anything else that you can find to identify them and their activities," I said.

"The files are straight from the government's hot little fist," Randy added, in a playful tone.

Lincoln took the USB without expression

"How much time does your mother have?" he asked.

"We're not sure," I replied, just managing to maintain self-control.

"Then I'd better get busy," he said, and walked off without another word.

I looked at Randy.

"That's his style, don't take it personally. He'll work day and night," Randy said, placing an arm about me supportively.

Randy suggested that we lunch near Yale but I wanted to see my mother and keep her up to date on events. We spoke little on the drive back to Greenwich.

"How much longer will you be involved with the Young boys?" I asked.

I wanted to change the subject, to stop obsessing about Lena's health. This worry had weighed on my mind since she told me of her medical condition. I was too young to lose her and she was too young to die.

"Not long. There's one more surveillance device to plant before I'm pulled out," Randy said.

His words didn't make me happy. Though being glad that the operation was nearly over, the expression that he chose implied that he considered himself an intelligence agent rather than a volunteer who need never look back. I hoped to marry a man with a safe job, not one who might make our children fatherless before they graduated from elementary school.

I said nothing and he noticed this.

"*What*?" he asked.

"Nothing."

"Come on. We promised to keep no secrets from each other," Randy insisted.

I pulled over as we entered Greenwich.

"I don't want you working in the intelligence service. It's too dangerous," I said, in an impassioned tone.

"I'm not! I'm just helping. Don't worry, I'm perfectly safe," Randy assured me.

Just weeks later, his words were to burn in my mind.

Chapter 97

Lena was hunched over paperwork when I arrived at her office. Twice widowed, she could now be considered a poster child for the unbalanced life. Working had become her life rather than enabling it. Her receptionist was away from her desk and I entered Lena's office without knocking. She looked up and smiled.

"How are you?" she asked.

"That's what I was about to ask you," I replied.

"Surviving, by trying not to think about possibilities. I was about to take a break. Care to join me?" she asked.

The hospital's cafeteria is a large windowed room with garden murals on the walls and club chairs in the corners. Only the food line distinguishes it from a high-class restaurant or expensively furnished home. After Lena bought the historic hospital she had it renovated so that patients might consider themselves as guests and not psychiatric cases.

"Have you found Blake?" Lena immediately asked.

Before replying, I took a spoonful of chocolate ice cream. This would be a long story.

"His name is now Creighton and not Blake. His family in on the run," I began.

I told her everything: the apparent link between Creighton's and the Young family which Randy had discovered; the government surveillance; Creighton's family's disappearance; and Randy's unusual friend, Lincoln.

Lena played with her cottage cheese salad when I finished speaking.

"There are some things in life that you wished you had never learned and now can't forget. What are the odds that he'll be found?" she finally asked.

"Peter obtained the government's files and Randy and Lincoln are studying them. Both are geniuses so if anyone can succeed they will. We can only wait," I said.

Though not wanting to give false hope, the word "wait" seemed to hang in the air. Time and her medical condition would move on despite our best efforts.

"How are you feeling?" I asked.

"Strange to say, though not well I do feel better. Two lab tests confirmed that I have cancer but the blood work and CT scan came back negative for abnormalities. There's reason for hope even if the oncologist insists that the lab work trumps the lack of other evidence."

"That's good news. What now?" I asked, with a smile.

"Now I await the final clinical opinion. My records were sent to another specialist who is a leader in the field. She'll tell me the good or bad news," Lena said.

"There's hope!" I said.

"Yes, my baby, there's always hope though death is nature's remedy for all things," Lena replied, in a somber tone.

Her depression had returned.

Chapter 98

Lena's depression affected me and I moped for the rest of the day. My family noticed and suggested that I try to relax. But how can I with all that's going on? I asked myself.

"When Nancy Drew is upset, she goes on vacation," Claudine, my baby sister, told me.

Nancy Drew, the famed fictional detective, is her hero and learning secrets has become her hobby. Still, Claudine was right.

"You're right. I'm leaving now!" I said.

"Where are you going?" Claudine asked.

I had little choice since I didn't want to be far from Lena.

"Not far, to a hotel in town where I can sit on the balcony and watch the boats," I replied.

"Is Randy going with you?" Claudine asked, with an aura of innocence.

"Go do your homework!" I ordered, with a smile, and quickly left the room.

Randy considered having a vacation a good idea too. Since my pregnancy scare, our mothers had accepted that we were sexually intimate but having sex at either home was still considered unacceptable. It was as if, on their premises, we became innocent children again.

Thus, the Delamar Hotel in Greenwich had become our adult playground. We could now afford this pleasure with the funds that I had gained in Berlin. We could have stayed at

Erika's home but that was hers and this was ours. Or as personal as a hotel room can be.

The Delamar is a small hotel with lovely complimentary touches: snacks, an evening reception, and a boat ride around the harbor. We accepted the snacks and ride but ignored the wine reception though Randy wanted to go. That was until I reminded him what he already knew: Mormons don't drink. I added that I didn't sleep with men who did and he didn't press the issue.

Our spacious 4th floor room had a sitting area on the balcony with a view of the harbor. After returning from the boat ride we ate at l'escale, the Mediterranean restaurant in the hotel.

Being obsessed with living a healthy lifestyle, I ordered for both of us and Randy didn't object. My taking over practical matters lets him concentrate on what he does best: being a genius.

When we began dating six years earlier, he would ignore his mother's order to get a haircut but accept mine. Still, being an individual matter, what is best for us won't necessarily work for you.

I ordered Georgette's Salad (kale, Brussels sprouts, quinoa, and more), Mediterranean Salmon which included minute ratatouille and chick pea, and spinach on the side. Randy choose the desserts which we shared: an apple tart and pumpkin cheesecake.

As beverage, I chose water and he had coffee. Mormons don't drink tea or coffee but Randy isn't Mormon and I don't impose my religious beliefs onto others. The issue of our children's religion we haven't yet worked out

Margaret in Manhattan

After returning to our room, we went immediately to bed and soon fell asleep. My dream which followed wasn't pleasant: I was back in Tokyo, tied naked on a table, awaiting death by torture as the red-hot tip of the soldering iron approached. The pounding on the door pulled us awake.

Chapter 99

As quickly as Randy awoke he fell back asleep. This was his habit and nothing short of an A-bomb or continued prodding would awaken him.

Though leaping from thc bed, I was still entrenched in my nightmare. The soldering iron approached and I had to escape. *There is no time, no time*, my racing mind told me.

I quickly slipped into a shirt, jeans, and boots. During combat, boots can be a weapon but I scanned the room for something better. My eyes latched onto the paring knife beside the hotel's complimentary cheese tray. It would have to do.

"I'm coming," I said loudly, and approached the door.

There, while turning the knob with my left hand, I kept a fighting grip on the knife in my right hand. With the door half-open, I thrust the knife toward the man's throat. But his firm hand stopped my killing strike and he slapped me hard. I fell back into the room–and became fully awake.

"*Dushka* (sweet, sincere one), did I hurt you," Borya said.

"Did I hurt *you*?" I asked, shaking my head.

"Have I not said that Margaret is dangerous?" Ivan said, with a small smile.

Ivan, a Russian military attaché, is another of my relatives. I had reacted in a deadly fashion when, in a Manhattan park, he had surprisingly embraced me from the rear.

Lee and Hedy (her birth name is Hedwig) were also there. Hedy is a shadowy figure of Germany's Federal Intelligence Service, the BND (Bundesnachrichtendienst). She is one of the 10% of their employees who are Bundeswehr soldiers employed by the Office for Military Sciences. We had met at one of Vladimir's parties in Berlin.

This would not be an ordinary meeting, I told myself. Despite their suave exteriors, Borya, Ivan, and Hedy had killed.

"Can we come in? Are you all right?" Ivan asked.

"I'm fine. When you banged on the door, I was having a nightmare about Tokyo. I'm sorry," I said.

"There's no need," Borya said, softly.

He and Ivan knew what happened there. It had resulted from a mistake, like what may have brought them here so early.

"Take a seat. I should probably wake Randy," I said.

"Yes, you had better," Borya said.

His tone lacked apology. Generals don't apologize to their soldiers before sending them into battle.

Chapter 100

Randy was dead to the world when I entered the bedroom. When I shook him gently, he tried to pull me back into bed.

"Get up. We have company," I said firmly.

"*Here*?" he asked.

"They're waiting for us. There must be an emergency," I said.

"*An emergency*?" Randy asked, still only half-awake.

"Something," I said.

I tossed underwear and socks from the drawer onto the bed. His jeans and a shirt followed.

"Dress quickly, you can shower later," I said, in my sternest no-nonsense tone.

"OK, mama," Randy said, with a grin, now fully awake.

I returned to the living room, being glad that I had taken a suite.

Our visitors sat silently, without a pretense of small talk. Our meeting would be all business.

I offered to order breakfast but they all refused.

"Randy will be out in a minute. What's going on?" I asked.

"It would be best to wait for him," Borya said.

He seemed to have taken charge. Randy took more than two minutes to dress but less than five. When he sat beside me on the sofa, Borya cleared his throat.

"Water?" I asked, to lessen the tension in the room.

"Please," he replied.

I got a bottle of Poland Spring Water from the mini-bar and handed it to him. He took a sip before turning toward us, seeming unsure how to begin.

"We've had new information. Hedy informed Vladimir who contacted me and I told Lee," Borya said

"It must be a matter of life and death to come so early," I said.

"More likely many deaths," Hedy said, in her perfect, unaccented English.

Chapter 101

Hedy's nervous tapping of her foot had told me that something serious happened. Her alarming words just added to this belief.

As Borya took charge, Randy sat up straighter and removed his hand from mine.

Borya turned toward Randy.

"When do intelligence services worry that a terror attack is imminent?" Borya asked him.

I didn't think that Randy knew anything about terrorism but he answered quickly.

"When there's increased internet chatter," he said.

"Yes, but they worry more when things become quiet. This means that messages are being passed which are so important that they're being delivered by hand, free from electronic interception. That's what's happening now and you, Randy, are dead center in the middle of it," Borya said.

Both Randy and I were too stunned to speak but I recovered first. I never liked Randy's involvement with the intelligence community and Hedy sensed my unspoken irritation.

"We've come to assure Randy's safety. Nothing will happen to him. He'll be pulled out at the first sign of danger," she said, in a reassuring tone.

I said nothing. Events rarely go as planned and words are cheap. But I didn't want to speak for Randy. Choosing his clothes was different from shaping his vocational path.

Moreover, I trusted Randy's judgement. Like some highly intelligent people, he had the ability to shut off all that is illogical in his thinking. Erika also has this ability. She can, almost by instinct, arrive at the correct decision while my mind is still lumbering along.

"It's obvious that you want something from me. What is it?" Randy asked.

Now, Lee spoke. Randy appeared to be the target at which each "heavy gun' took aim in turn.

"We need your help a little longer. The man you identified at the Young's apartment is a person of interest," Lee said.

"Why is he *a person of interest*"? Randy asked.

There seemed a reluctance to answer but Borya finally spoke.

"He's a renegade Russian scientist, a traitor without scruples who sells his expertise to the highest bidder. We would like to settle the score but have been forbidden to act in America," Borya said.

We all knew what that meant. A Russian assassination on American soil would doom any hope of improved American-Russian relations. This man's death wasn't worth that outcome.

"What do you want me to do?" Randy asked.

"A telephone intercept revealed that there will be a family gathering which this man will attend. It'll be in upstate New York and we want you there," Lee said.

Chapter 102

I gripped Randy's hand and my voice was thick as I spoke. They would *not* have the father of our yet-to-be-conceived children killed through some dumb plan. My t-shirt was bought for me by Randy in Austin. It fit the moment and read, emblazoned in large red letters, "I can be a real Texas bitch. Try me."

"Randy is an amateur. Are you out of your collective minds?" I asked, angrily.

The room was silent until Borya looked directly at me and spoke.

"Come, let's speak privately," he said, indicating the bedroom.

Borya's nickname is Lucifer and people listen when he speaks. I followed him into the bedroom.

There, he sat and motioned for me to do so.

"The *person of interest* is an expert in producing VX, the deadliest nerve agent ever developed. It was recently used to murder Kim Jong Nam, the half-brother of North Korea's dictator. It was also used in a Tokyo attack by a religious cult in 1995.

"There are indications that an attack in planned with the Young parents being involved. I normally wouldn't permit Randy to be involved but there is no one else. He has entrée into the family and is trusted by them," Borya said.

I gave in. There was no way for me to win this argument. I would lose even if I won since Randy would be furious. He would blame me for having sabotaged his chance to be a hero. He had devoured books about the Navy SEALS for years.

"OK, with one condition," I said, grudgingly.

Borya's mask of compassion vanished. He wasn't used to be bargained with.

"What's that?" he asked.

"I go with him," I said, in my firmest tone.

Chapter 103

Borya nodded agreement. He didn't like my condition but had no choice for he recognized my influence over Randy. If Randy went ahead without my blessing, he would behave half-heartedly and likely fail. Having my cooperation was crucial.

"Margaret will accompany Randy," Borya said, tersely, as we re-entered the living room.

"No way!" Randy asserted.

"Yes, way! I'm more experienced and won't have you going alone," I stormed back, looking him directly in the eye.

The others watched what, in another circumstance, would have been a lover's spat. Lee's comment settled the atmosphere.

"Let's figure out how this can be done. Have the Young parents ever seen you?" he asked.

"No, but one of their bodyguards did. We had a brief meeting in Central Park," I replied.

"We'll change your appearance and create a good reason for you to accompany Randy," Lee said.

"Because I'm pregnant?" I suggested.

Hedy added the first smile to our discussion.

"Of course! A pregnant woman doesn't want to leave her man and is considered needy. You'd be viewed as an *almost mother,* not a potential enemy. This would give you freedom to look around while Randy plays daddy-to-be with their kids."

I smiled too. I liked it.

"How do we keep in touch?" I asked.

"We have phones," Randy suggested.

"We'll need more than that. Signals for when we've accomplished what we came for or are in trouble," I said.

Randy stared at me with disbelief and Hedy turned toward him.

"This is serious stuff. What you're doing could get you killed," she said, though in a casual tone.

We were given two signals. Daily phone calls were to be made to "my mother," supposedly to reassure her about my health. When the assignment was completed, whatever it was, I would say, "My baby is growing." If we needed rescue, I was to say, "I felt a kick but it's so early."

"And don't worry, the cavalry will come a-galloping," Lee said, with a smile.

Later that day, I still wondered if Lee had been honest or was simply making a joke.

Chapter 104

Almost immediately, the atmosphere in the room had changed from confrontation to collaboration. Two goals were voiced: to change my appearance, and to educate us about what we were to look for. Randy's mind latched onto the second goal at once. Though computer science was his field, he was more familiar with technical terms than me despite my Barnard chemistry courses. I read newspapers to relax while he reads up on science.

"How much do you know about VX and its production?" Hedy asked.

"Just that it's a nerve gas," I replied, and Randy remained silent.

"OK. VX interferes with the signals that pass between the brain and the muscles. If your nerve impulse tells a muscle to contract, you must turn it off lest the muscle stay contracted. The one that kills is a spasm of the diaphragm so that you can't breathe. You die of asphyxiation," Hedy said.

"VX works through skin contact or breathing. Though all nerve agents accomplish the same, VX is particularly dangerous because it's heavier. It settles on the on the ground and could make an area unusable.

"VX is so dangerous that just a tiny drop is lethal. All countries except North Korea agreed to destroy their stockpile of VX as part of the Chemical Weapons Convention of 1993."

"Once one country uses it, the Red Line is crossed," Lee added, and Hedy nodded agreement.

"How hard is it to make?" Randy asked.

"I'll go into that after you hear the story of a Japanese cult, Aum Shinrikyo. I must leave in a few minutes so I'll make it brief," Lee said.

"This cult didn't control its own territory like ISIL, the Islamic State, does, but it had the advantage of being ignored by the Japanese police. It first spent thirty million dollars to build a laboratory to make anthrax into a weapon. After failing at that, they succeeded with VX. They killed more than twenty people and injured thousands more before being caught. They wasted money on the anthrax since VX is far easier to make," Lee said.

After that alarming statement, Lee returned the platform to Hedy and left the room.

Chapter 105

"VX is easier to make than anthrax, and is safer to store with simple precautions. It's a liquid at normal temperature and, like water, evaporates quickly," Hedy continued.

"How many people can it kill?" I asked.

"That depends on how much there is. Five quarts of VX could kill everyone on a subway train if they couldn't leave. It doesn't smell so people don't know what's happening until it's too late. It's relatively cheap to make too," Hedy replied.

"How much would it cost?" I asked.

"A few hundred thousand dollars for the lab equipment, which is pretty basic."

"How is it made? What should we look for?" I asked.

"What's the science?" Randy asked.

"All that I know is what was recently crammed into me by an expert. In the 1930s, while searching for pesticides, German scientists discovered lethal molecules called organophosphates. The Nazis recognized its use as a weapon but feared that using it would provoke a counterattack.

"To produce VX, one first makes a chemical called DF."

"Methylphosphonyl difluoride," Randy blurted.

"Correct. DF can eat through glass and, if mixed with water, it releases deadly hydrofluoric acid. By itself it can last for years until being mixed with isopropyl alcohol, the rubbing alcohol that can be bought in any drugstore. Mix these two and you get VX and death," Hedy said.

"Like other nerve agents, VX works by blocking the enzyme, cholinesterase. With cholinesterase being unable to work, muscle cells can't turn themselves off and continually fire until destroying themselves.

"VX can be produced using widely sold chemicals: methanol, alcohol's lethal cousin, and phosphorus trichloride. Heating these two together produces trimethylphosphine and getting from that to DF takes only three more steps.

"All this takes just college chemistry knowledge. Governments can't stop the sale of basic industrial chemicals nor of the required lab and safety equipment: mass spectrometer, fume hoods, beakers, pipettes, Bunsen burners, respirators, full-body chemical handling suits," Hedy said.

The room became silent as we digested the horror of what Hedy had described.

"Your job is to discover what's going on so we can stop it," Borya finally said.

Chapter 106

After everyone except Hedy had left, I ordered breakfast. It wasn't the weekend that I had planned for Randy and me. My anxiety shuttled from worrying about Lena's illness to the danger that approached.

No matter how elaborate were Lee's precautions, Randy and I would be risking out lives. Earning a statue in Greenwich Park ("To Memorialize Greenwich's Two Biggest Idiots") hadn't been in my plans for our future. Hedy sensed my distress.

"It's normal to worry. Anxiety keeps the wits sharp," she said.

"It's our brains that aren't sharp for agreeing," I replied, nastily.

Randy stared at me but Hedy didn't reply. No one spoke again until after the food arrived and we were eating. Eating settles the nerves.

"How do I get us invited upstate?" Randy asked.

Hedy smiled at his question. She had remained behind to teach us spy craft.

"You'll understand better if I tell you a story," Hedy said.

We leaned back, munched, and waited.

"The BND (Germany's Federal Intelligence Service) once received word that a major terrorist was in Berlin. We knew who he was but hadn't enough evidence to arrest him. He lived above a small internet café and spent much of his time on one of their computers or eating.

Margaret in Manhattan

"We sent in an Arabic speaking agent who was instructed not to approach the terrorist. Instead, he should simply hang out at the café. We hoped that they would become friends. For days, they sat at neighboring computers, each doing their own thing. Gradually, they began exchanging a few words, first about computers and then on world events.

"Two weeks later they ate at a restaurant where my agent insisted on paying their bill. He said that the terrorist could pay for their next meal. Only months later was enough evidence gained for successful prosecution.

"Gaining information isn't about asking questions. It's spending so much time with an individual that they willingly reveal something to you.

"If you get people comfortable enough, they'll soon become boastful and reveal all that you need. Angle the questions right, never hitting straight on or hammering away at something. Then circle back to the matter at another time and you'll eventually get it all," Hedy said.

Randy and I looked at each other. We were impressed.

Chapter 107

"Do you have any questions so far?" Hedy asked.

Both Randy and I shook our heads and waited for Hedy to continue. But she seemed satisfied to munch on her cream-cheese smeared/cinnamon-raison bagel and let her lessons sink in.

My thinking turned to Randy and how ill-equipped he was for spy duty. Randy is a good person but immature regarding certain moral issues. He has a personality that seeks explanations and excuses for the evil that people can commit. He doesn't understand that the snakes of the world respect only strength and the will to use it.

I become almost awkwardly protective when I see him. But this was not the feeling that one should have considering the covert world that we had entered.

Peering into the glass of my latest health food kick (organic black cherry juice) and deep in thought, I barely recognized that Hedy had begun speaking again.

"You seem far away, Margaret," she said, with a smile.

"I'm just worrying," I replied.

Randy took my hand supportively. I smiled at him but my worry remained.

"What's the next step?" I asked.

Hedy smeared orange marmalade on her bagel and took another bite before answering. It was as if my question concerned the most ordinary matter in the world.

"Next, you both relax for the rest of the day. Take a boat ride or see a movie. Act like the young loving couple that you are," Hedy said.

A couple that may be dead in a week, I thought, but didn't say.

"A movie sounds good. How about coming with us?" I asked.

Hedy hesitated before answering, perhaps thinking that she had more important things to do but also recognizing our need for support.

"That sounds wonderful!" she said, with enthusiasm.

Her emotion sounded genuine but I knew that she was a good actress. My gloom returned and this may have been why I made a dumb comment. I was starting to lose it.

"Show Randy your weapons!" I blurted.

After a brief stare, Hedy smiled and complied. The condemned prisoner having their final wish satisfied, I thought.

Hedy removed three weapons from her body: a lightweight .38 caliber Smith & Wesson with a two-inch barrel, a compact .45 caliber Kimber SIS Ultra, and a pocket knife with a serrated blade. One gun was drawn from a bra holster, the second from an ankle holster, and the switchblade came from her pocket.

"Always Be Prepared" was Hedy's adage for life. She had been a bullied teenager until the day that her tormentor grabbed her crotch. The following day she broke his arms with a hockey bat. After newspaper coverage of her arrest and expulsion from school, her family received a dinner invitation from an admiring Army recruiter.

Margaret in Manhattan

"Which gun do I get?" Randy asked, admiringly.

I stared since I'm the gifted shot.

"You get me," I said.

Chapter 108

The movie that Hedy and I wanted to see was the Academy Award winner, *Manchester by the Sea*. Randy preferred *John Wick: Chapter 2*, in which a retired hitman squares off against deadly killers. Though voting two to one for *Manchester*, we saw *John Wick*. Like I said, the condemned get their choice even if their fate reflected their decision.

Still, I had felt unable to refuse. Years before, Ivan had saved my life in London and, later, that of my friend in New York City. He deserved my loyalty.

Yet despite all the professional assistance given us, I couldn't shed the conviction that Randy was heading for disaster. His merciful personality made him the perfect victim for anyone who wished him ill. I dreaded the moment when I learned of his death.

Hedy had seen the first *John Wick* movie and compared them as we sat in Starbucks after the viewing. She felt that the sequel was inferior. While the first film had a lightness that softened the slaughter, the second was more solemn, weighed down by the philosophy that more bodies are better. Wick's sliding a knife from his back pocket reminded me of Hedy's switchblade. I hunger for romance and get terror, I told myself, unhappily.

But romance did come. For whatever reason, perhaps from fear, that night turned into an orgy. Having sex four times in one night might not be a world record but it was for Randy and me. Afterward, soaked with perspiration and burning hot, I could only kiss him and say, "Thank you," before falling into a dreamless sleep.

Margaret in Manhattan

The next day, as Randy studied eavesdropping gadgets with Lee, Hedy changed my appearance. Seeing myself in the mirror, I realized that I would have to think up an explanation for my family.

My long red hair was gone. I was now a short-haired brunette with fittingly colored eyelashes and suitable eyeliner and lipstick. My parents would barely recognize me. With my small breasts and thin butt, I feared that I looked like a boy. How will tonight's sex be? I wondered.

Chapter 109

My lawyer-father once said that it never pays to take someone for how they seem even if that's the only thing you have to go on. I must have been nervous because, while undressing that night, I had an unwelcome thought: If that night's sex was better than the previous night, was it because I now resembled a boy? If so, might this indicate something about Randy's sexual preference? Years from now, after our children were born, would he suddenly assert that he was gay?

In the morning, I recognized that my worry had been dim-witted. Whether from stress or tiredness, we didn't have sex that night. Well, married couples don't have sex every night either, I consoled myself, with information gained from an Internet search.

After breakfast, Randy and I returned to our homes. Despite our independent ways, we still had families to answer to. And it was Sunday which is church going day in my family but not Randy's.

Their faith is science while mine is a combination of Mormonism and Santeria. But this is acceptable, Mother Marie, a Santeria priestess, had told me for "The Gods are not jealous."

Nor, I felt, would any just God reject my prayer for its goal was noble. But a later thought reduced this reassurance: good intentions and sound plans don't guarantee success.

During each Mormon service, several congregants share a painful experience they overcame. Was it mere chance that one of these stories seemed directed at me? I asked myself.

Chapter 110

"Sometimes a hero is just a person who keeps on going, doing what needs to be done even when their spirits are weak," said the speaker.

"I'm an electrician and was working outside a house when I heard a woman screaming. She was a jogger being attacked by a pit bull and two of her two mixed-breed offspring. The dogs were atop her and turned on me when I tried to help her up. I managed to drag the woman into my van with the dogs in pursuit.

"She had wounds to the bone on her ankle and elbow, bites on her face, and was losing blood. When paramedics arrived, alerted by neighbors' calls to 911, the dogs targeted them before retreating into the woods. The woman was hospitalized for four days and I needed surgery on my injured elbow."

His was an inspiring story but it was his last words, a quote from Lao Tzu, that moved me the most: "Being deeply loved by someone gives you strength; loving someone deeply gives you courage."

Randy loved me deeply and was risking his life for me. I loved him deeply and would protect him as best I could.

Everyone's weekend routine is different. Erika, her father, and his current girlfriend have Sunday brunch at a local restaurant. Randy's family–his father is an over-worked surgeon–relax at home.

My family has brunch. There's nothing special about it, just our favorites: meat loaf for the others and soy-chicken for me, assorted vegetables, poppy-seed rolls, and peanut butter cookies for dessert.

My fifteen-year-old sister, Melanie, had done the baking. It was long obvious to all that my birth mother's culinary gene must have been deficient.

But it is our conversation and not the food which is important. We can never be sure what topic will grab our attention. On some days, it's one of my father's law cases. That day, it was Melanie's question.

"What should a girl do when her ex said he was going to kill her and had already decided what to do with her body?" she asked.

Eating stopped as we awaited anyone's responce.

Chapter 111

All eyes turned toward Melanie. She looked stricken and I understood. What her friend revealed was shared in confidence and Melanie had just blared it out. Moreover, it wasn't the kind of thing that she could take back by saying "I was joking" or something like that. No one would believe her.

"You'd better tell us," my father said, softly.

My mother suggested that Claudine go to her room but my father disagreed.

"The earlier she learns what to do in such situations, the safer she will be," he said.

He turned toward Melanie who slowly began speaking.

"She said that he was two years older and great looking. He was her first boyfriend and everything was perfect. She felt important and special though it might have been his bad-boy personality that appealed to her," Melanie said.

"Some girls find tacky boys exciting," Melody interjected.

I wondered if her observation was based on personal experience but she didn't speak more and Melanie continued.

"Rumors circulated that he was cheating on her. When she tried to talk to him about it, he got angry. At a school dance, he refused to take pictures because he didn't like what she wore. Her friends were embarrassed and she didn't know what to say.

"After that, she did whatever he wanted to avoid arguments. She wouldn't ask questions that she wasn't sure he would answer or make plans with friends until checking with him. She loved him and didn't feel that a fight was worth it.

"That was until she realized that she had changed and was no was longer the girl that she had been. So she broke up with him but agreed to stay friends.

"While they were hanging out at his home, she discovered him looking through her phone. When she asked what he was doing, he grabbed her by the neck and choked her. He said he was going to kill her and knew how to make her body disappear.

"Then he let her go and started crying. He apologized and begged her not to tell anyone and said that he'd never act that way again. She didn't tell but two days ago he did the same thing. She's wearing a scarf to hide the marks on her neck."

Silence again settled over the table. Now it was Claudine who broke it.

"He's a weirdian," she said.

Her made-up word didn't produce the smile that it usually does.

"You haven't shared two important facts," my father said.

"What are they?" Melanie asked, tremblingly.

"The names of your friend and the boy," my father replied.

Chapter 112

Melanie looked torn. While understanding why our father had asked for the names, she had promised confidentially to her friend. Which, I felt, she shouldn't have since privacy doesn't exist in life-or-death issues. Being a lawyer's child, Melanie knew this. She accepted the inevitable and told.

"I must make a phone call," my father said, and left the table.

It was obvious that he would phone the girl's parents. What followed would be up to them.

When he returned, we looked at him expectantly.

"I spoke first with her father and then with Sergeant Alamo. It's not a matter that can be kept within a family. Even if your friend is safe, who is to say what will happen to the next girl that he takes up with. The boy needs professional help and maybe more," my father said.

"*More*?" Melanie asked, anxiously.

"If the parents press charges, he'll likely wind up in Family Court. There, he could be sentenced to probation and required mental health treatment. But if he's treated as an adult…"

My father left this severer outcome unspecified.

"I feel awful," Melanie said.

"You shouldn't. You might have saved a girl's life and the boy's future," Melody said.

I agreed, and doubted that anyone wouldn't.

"Well, he is a weirdian," Claudine repeated, with a sigh.

"Is everyone ready for dessert?" my mother asked, brightly.

Her question caused a welcome change to the atmosphere in the room.

Melanie's story wasn't the only surprise that day for the doorbell rang as my mother went to the kitchen. Moments later, Erika and her father, Hamilton, who prefers to be called Harry, entered the dining room.

"Would you have space for us?" Erika asked.

"Absolutely!" my father beamed, and rose to bring over more chairs.

"Have you eaten?" my mother asked.

"Please, don't go to any trouble. We're just here for a visit," Erika said.

Then, noting Melanie's downcast expression, she added, "It seems we're interrupting."

"A problem with Melanie's friend that's now settled," my father said, hurriedly.

"We hope!" Melanie blurted.

Erika smiled and said nothing. She sensed that, whatever the issue, it wasn't their business.

Chapter 113

For the next half-hour, the parents spoke of local issues: pesticides had been found at fields surrounding the Greenwich High School six years earlier and it would take another four years to clear it; the recent blizzard, and emergency warming shelters which had been set up for town employees who needed to work around the clock to keep roads clear; and more.

"Carbon monoxide incidents at two homes might have been deadly," Harry said.

My parents nodded politely as the rest of us tried to look interested. What they shared was important but these matters lay far from our minds. A murderous boyfriend they weren't.

Erika followed me when I went to the kitchen to get more cookies. There, we huddled.

"We're glad to see you but what's really going on?" I asked.

"What happened at today's brunch. We usually eat at L'Escale but my father said that he wanted something different since today would be a celebration. We went to Thomas Henkelmann," Erika said.

I waited but nothing else came.

"*So?*" I asked.

"It's a wonderful restaurant. The same people have worked there for years and the beautiful surroundings remind you of what Greenwich must have been like in the 1920s. They greeted us with a smile that even excused my sneakers and jeans."

Clearly, despite the restaurant's elegance, *something* important had happened during the brunch. I learned from my lawyer-father that when someone is spilling their story, it's best not to interrupt. I listened silently, knowing that I would eventually learn what occurred.

"We enjoyed the foie gras trio plate and my lamb and their sole were cooked perfectly. Each was presented with just the right accompaniments. And the desserts were perfect."

Despite my dad's advice, I couldn't contain myself.

"That's interesting but what went wrong?" I asked.

"Nothing, except that the main event didn't come off as my father had intended," Erika said.

A devious smile lit her face, and I waited.

Chapter 114

Erika is one of the cleverest teenagers in America. For her to get *that* look meant that she must have done something exceptional, and which she hungered to share.

"You know about Brittany?" she asked.

How could I not? Brittany was her father's latest trophy girlfriend and Erika had been raging against her since they met. Being twenty-years younger and a celebrated model, she was exactly the kind of woman that her father would fall for and be exactly the wrong choice too.

Erika's mother had been an intellectual, a doctor. She and Erika's older sister were murdered by a business rival of her father when Erika was a child and her father had never fully recovered from his wife's loss. Erika had suffered with him during the troubled years when he taught math at Columbia University. That was before he became a Wall Street wunderkind and billionaire.

What Harry needed as a mate was a highly intelligent woman to share his worries and to help parent Erika, as much as she would allow. Erika would be a handful for any parent.

"Do you remember how they met?" Erika asked.

It would be hard to forget. During a trip into Manhattan, he for business meetings and she for shopping, Harry and Erika had arranged to meet for lunch at Bergdorf Goodman, a few blocks from Trump Tower. Afterward, Harry accompanied her to the lingerie department for a final purchase. While waiting as she shopped, he was fussed over by sales clerks who recognized him as a valued customer.

Margaret in Manhattan

Harry was standing by the bra counter when Brittany asked him to hold several bras for her while she completed shopping. She was beautiful enough to get away with it and their first date soon followed. That was a month ago and Erika had hated her ever since.

"Sleeping with Brittany is one thing but marrying her? When he showed me the engagement ring, a platinum Infinity Twist with a three-carat diamond, I knew that the time for action had arrived. He couldn't see that her only interest in him was his money.

"Marriage to her would destroy him during the brief time that it lasted and he couldn't tolerate the trauma of a divorce and second loss."

"So?" I asked, trying to hurry the story along.

"I hired a detective to check her out and he was well worth it. At the brunch, just as my dad was about to pop the question, I asked Brittany, sweetly: 'Though there's still six months to go, have you and your lover chosen your baby's name?'

"Brittany's face turned red with fury, understanding swept my father's face, and he and I made the quickest exit ever from a restaurant."

Chapter 115

Erika's story gave me a much-needed laugh. She was more relaxed too and, when we returned to the living room, I saw that Harry's face was less drawn. He needed a good wife and would choose one if Erika had anything to do with it.

"Harry seemed stressed," my mother remarked, after they left.

"He just broke-up with his latest girlfriend," I said.

"How sad," my mother said.

"How fortunate. She was the worst kind of gold-digger," I replied.

I was quiet for the rest of the day, smiling and making brief responses but not really being there. My mind was on Randy and what could happen over the following week. We should have been together but, as I said, we both have family obligations.

My lawyer-father frequently advises his clients not to worry until they have something to worry about. I tried to follow this good advice but couldn't. Among other things, I still hadn't decided whether to study at Barnard or in Berlin the next school term.

Erika had noticed my upset and her last words before leaving were, "My father looks screwed-up but you look like a God-damn train wreck."

I used the usual excuse of a headache, left the family, and went to nap in my room. Odd thoughts came to mind. First, Hedy's statement, "When you want something, you first try treachery and then weird sexual offers." Then something that my older sister, Melody, once said, "Don't be confused between building a family and having fun."

I determined to keep the first in mind and to attempt the second. Life is a battle, I told myself, with nature having two primary rules: to act with resolve, and to seek to understand.

While relaxed in this thoughtful mood, I managed to nap until a dream startled me awake. Randy, me, and two children were walking toward a small house in a snow-covered landscape. "We'll miss you," one boy said. "I'll still visit you in New York," Randy replied. "No, the dead don't travel," the child replied, sadly.

Chapter 116

The problem with taking a nap is that it screws up your sleep schedule. When I awoke, I needed someone to talk to. I felt terrified, having the lingering sense of impending doom from my nightmare. But, at that time, everyone seemed asleep.

Eating relieves anxiety, for me as for many people. I went downstairs and left the kitchen with a nearly full box of Fig Newtons. Then, hearing voices, I walked to my father's home-office.

The room was empty but his laptop was open on the desk. He had apparently stepped out for a minute and the voices came from a video that was playing. It took a moment for me to recognize what I was seeing. I'm not naive but the scene was shocking and particularly when viewed in my home.

In the video were two naked people: a man who was standing, and a teenager who lay face down with her hands bound to a bed. The man was forcing anal sex onto her and she screamed from pain. After finishing, he slapped her face hard. "Oh, daddy, wasn't I a good girl?" she asked, with a look of fear that seemed feigned. "*Good? Good? I'll show you!*" the man screamed, and began beating her buttocks with a small belt.

I was so entranced by the video that I didn't hear my father's approach. Without saying a word, he closed the lid of the laptop. I looked up at him, mutely. The presence of S&M porn on the Internet wasn't surprising but that my father enjoyed it––*and in our home*–was. I looked away from him.

"Interesting," I remarked, inanely, still looking away.

Margaret in Manhattan

"I was just looking for you. The man in the video is a new client who is being blackmailed. I was thinking of hiring Randy to study the video and discover who sent it."

Chapter 117

I took a long time to respond to what my father wanted. *Too long*, so he would get the message.

"*What?*" he asked, finally.

"He can't do it," I said, flatly.

"You've said that his Yale computer professor described him as 'a genius.' At the very least he would be helpful," my father objected.

"It's not that. Randy shocks easily and I don't want him seeing that video. I try to keep him away from nastiness. But I can suggest another person, someone that Randy has described as being a better hacker than even him. Vladimir used him for a tough job and he came through," I said.

"*Great!* What's his name?" my father asked.

"It's not that easy. Randy met him during a conference in Austin. He's Russian and is now back home. He's also expensive, and has worked for the Russian Mafia and the SVR (Russia's Foreign Intelligence Service)," I said.

"Will he keep things confidential?" my father asked.

"Absolutely, or Vladimir wouldn't have used him. What's your budget?"

"There is none. Offer whatever you think will attract him. We'll wire him one-third as down payment plus travel expenses," my father said.

"Your client must be important, and wealthy," I said.

"You didn't recognize him in the video?"

"I wasn't looking at his face."

My father named a recent blockbuster movie.

"Of course, it's *him*. And he's always shown as a salt-of-the-earth family guy," I said, with a smile.

"That's Hollywood for you," my father said.

"There could be a movie script in this," I said.

"Yes," my father agreed.

Neither of us was smiling.

Chapter 118

Alyosha was the Russian hacker's name and, despite his nationality, he behaved no differently from the American hackers that I had met. He worked around the clock, slurped Coke like it was on the verge of being rationing, and was addicted to greasy fast-food. He was also, in his narrow sphere of work, considered a genius.

Thanks to Alyosha's help, the kidnapped son of Texas' Attorney General had been rescued, unharmed, and his drug cartel kidnappers were brought to justice.

Alyosha had proven to be honest and dependable. So, despite his criminal and Russia spy entanglements, I hadn't hesitated to recommend him to my father. "He could find cheaper help but no one better," Randy later said.

But hiring him proved difficult. Though he had recently traveled to America without problem, the tightened American visa restrictions had aroused his fear of an FBI sting operation and arrest. He wouldn't leave Russia without an ironclad guarantee of safety–which my father couldn't gain.

Randy suggested that Alyosha had no need to travel here. The data that he needed to conduct his investigation could be sent to him using encrypted E-mail and Skype and this was done.

Payment was wired electronically into Alyosha's off-shore bank account in Malta. The money was probably re-wired elsewhere, to multiple locations, soon after it arrived. Even with his powerful friends, Alyosha took elaborate security precautions. But these would not save him were the drug cartel to become aware of his role in the death of their workers.

Margaret in Manhattan

I never asked my father how the case was progressing. I didn't want to know. I had enough worries and the rescue of a sleazy actor would never be one of them.

I spent those final days practicing my lines, avoiding questions from my family about my changed appearance, and waiting to perform with Randy, my co-star in our upcoming drama.

Randy phoned me late one evening. The family's upstate vacation was set for the following weekend. We would soon be onstage.

Chapter 119

As Vladimir and so many generals have said, plans don't usually work out as intended. For our protection and more, Lee had secretly affixed a GPS device to the Young's car. But, at the last minute, Mr. Young had decided to rent a large four-wheel drive SUV. We would be together from Friday night dinner in their apartment until our return from upstate New York.

After Randy and I arrived at their apartment Friday afternoon, my introduction was made. Hedy had advised me that the most effective lies answer questions that haven't yet been asked and I followed her advice during dinner.

Randy had told them that I was vegetarian. This wasn't a problem since many Chinese dishes combine vegetables and fish and I love both.

As entree, we had Thousand Year Egg which turned out to be less odd that it sounds. It consisted, I was told, of duck eggs preserved in a mixture of rice husk, clay, lime, salt, and ash for weeks or months. The dark brown egg had a green yolk and tasted OK.

Next came Peking Roast Duck. It is considered one of China's national dishes having been around since the Imperial age. There was chocolate sorbet for dessert.

I followed another of Hedy's suggestions: to take Randy's hand often, apparently impulsively, since "nothing seems more innocent than young love."

I let Randy do the talking during dinner. He spoke with the children about the Raspberry Pi micro-computers that they were building and told amusing stories about his fellow students at Yale.

Dinner passed harmoniously, as did our later conversation in the living room. Hedy had also advised me that an innocent topic to establish my bone fides could be my alleged pregnancy and about this I gushed.

"I was *so* excited to learn I was pregnant but I *still* can't imagine having *a baby*. My first symptom was the *strangest* taste in my mouth before I even knew. I did the test in the middle of the night and though it was so late I still phoned *everybody*," I said.

Though the children looked bored, Mr. and Mrs. Young smiled with understanding. No real Valley Girl would have sounded more natural.

Chapter 120

The SUV had three rows of seats and plenty of room. Mr. and Mrs. Young sat in the front row, their sons sat in the second row, and Randy and I sprawled in the third row. My anxiety was an additional passenger.

We spoke little during the two-and-one-half-hour drive. While their mother looked out the window, the boys played *Resident Evil 7,* a survival video game that I wouldn't have let my children play. But Mrs. Young might not have known. Were my parents aware of all that I had done, they would have more gray hairs than they do.

I held Randy's hand as we dozed. We had slept poorly the night before. Having sex would have relaxed us except for the thought that our performance would be preserved on video.

My body's lurch as we left the interstate awoke me and I looked around. The exit sign said "Woodstock." Mr. Young now addressed us for the first since we left Manhattan. It sounded like a tour guide comment and intended to relax us.

"The 1969 Woodstock Festival wasn't held here but in Bethel which is in a neighboring county," he said.

"I didn't know though *everyone* has heard of the Woodstock Festival," I said, brightly, in my best Valley Girl tone.

The silence had gotten to me. I welcomed conversation to reduce my anxiety but that was the parents' last comment until we reached our destination.

The last part of the journey was on a poorly kept, narrow gravel road. No surveillance car could have followed us without being seen. That the car which Lee had fitted with a tracking device had not been used had spooked me. Were we suspected or were the parents merely being cautious? I wondered.

Randy was jumpy too. Apart from his Navy SEAL fantasies of being a hero, he was outside his element. Babying a computer in a climate-controlled office was his routine, not deception and danger. I had promised myself to protect him but the plan had already gone wrong.

Chapter 121

The house was probably what a ski chalet should look like. I didn't know since I had never gone skiing. It was a two-story, pitched roof construction with seven bedrooms and four bathrooms. It might have gotten its "ski chalet" status because of the plentiful snow in the area.

Racks by the door held ski equipment which attracted no glances. They seemed decor, like the color-coordinated, leather-bound books in the libraries of non-reading families which are acquired for decoration rather than use.

Upon arriving, a middle-aged couple, Mr., and Mrs. Alpert, greeted us. They were introduced as the cook and handyman. Hands were shaken with the wife making a practiced smile and her husband granting a nod.

Despite their Anglican name and language fluency, they spoke with a guttural accent and English didn't seem their native language. This might have accounted for the food which was basically German and what I had eaten in Berlin.

Our first day there was spent doing what we had done in Manhattan: eating and lazing around. No one suggested skiing, Randy battled the boys with Resident Evil video play and Mr. and Mrs. Young read.

There was little else to do. The house was out-of-range of cable TV, and cellular service, to create a Hotspot Internet connection, was uncertain. I read too, having downloaded several novels onto my Kindle app before leaving Manhattan. And looking for a pleasant spot to read, gave me a believable excuse to explore the house.

Margaret in Manhattan

I didn't expect us to be so isolated. My image of skiing came from magazine photos of smiling people trudging the slopes, not huddling indoors over video games and books.

I had been instructed to look for what would be out-of-place in a home: chemical apparatus, or the germ warfare ingredients which had been described. To do this while awaiting the arrival of Borya's "person of interest."

Chapter 122

While Randy and the kids played video games, the parents did their thing, and I had my reading. I felt tense and bored.

The atmosphere was odd, one in which people seemed frozen into keeping busy. Though supposedly a vacation, Mr. and Mrs. Young didn't seem to be enjoying themselves, and there weren't even the expected smiles for guests.

I wondered why Randy and I had been invited until a possible explanation occurred to me. A non-skiing family in a ski area during ski season might look suspicious but not with young people around. Moreover, Randy could keep the boys busy as crucial events happened.

Meanwhile, I gurgled on in Valley Girl fashion about innocent topics. These mostly involved the house and its furnishings, which were impressive.

The house was in the 18th century style and like many of the rambling structures that I had seen in London the past summer. It was painted a monstrous shade of green with red trim and roof. Furnishings were Victorian with comfortable high-back chairs and settees. Every room had a working fireplace, carpeted floors, and flowered wallpaper or draping.

There was a third-floor roof deck for sunset gazing and a front porch where an English High Tea might be served during the summer.

Though ideal for a romantic getaway, Randy became increasingly nervous as the hours passed and sex was far from his mind. Still, I pressed that remedy and it worked. Early the next morning, Randy turned toward me with a smile.

Margaret in Manhattan

"You *raped* me!" he said.

But he *was* more relaxed.

Chapter 123

I began searching the house. If discovered, I would say that I was seeking a comfortable place to read. The house was larger than I had thought for it had a locked door that seemed to lead to an entire other wing.

But I couldn't investigate further at that moment since the house had rigid rules. Meals were at set times with everyone expected to be present. It was like being at my home. Still, later would be a better time to act and I needed equipment too.

Government bureaucrats are cautious and with good reason. Gaining bad publicity could result in their dismissal and loss of pension. They're not used to private employment where jobs change frequently and one lasting more than five years is considered lifetime.

For them, the worst publicity is being responsible for a civilian's harm, which Randy and I were. Thus, Lee's instructions had been strict: we were to carry no weapons or anything concealed. Our only role at this house was as innocent guests enjoying a weekend. Sure!

Borya had no such concerns and followed his own rules. The most important of these is that success excuses all mistakes. Two days before, he had taken me aside.

"Don't worry about what you must do. People flock to the side of winners," he said.

"But what if I lose?" I asked, with a slight smile.

"Don't lose!" Borya replied, without a smile.

Margaret in Manhattan

I needed no training with the PSS, the Russian 7.62mm small, silenced pistol that he handed me. I had been instructed on it before. Learning the lock-picking gadget was easy. It was simple enough to be used by an idiot, which my involvement in this mission had been causing me to think that I was.

Chapter 124

I hadn't been a total beginner when Hedy brought out the lock-picking kit. Picking locks had been Randy's hobby since childhood. He told me that this recreation had enthusiasts ranging from King Louis XVI of France to the eminent physicist, Richard Feynman. Feynman is one of Randy's heroes.

Randy had long since given up this hobby in favor of hacking computer networks which he found more challenging. Like every girlfriend, I endure his pastimes and learn from them.

Hobby lockpickers use the same tools as burglars: picks, jigglers, the bump key, and the torsion wrench. Because learning to use these well would have taken more time than we had, Hedy provided me with two gadgets: an electric Snap Gun, which causes the lock pins to vibrate while a torsion wrench is used; and a Tubular Lock Pick, which is inserted into a lock and can open it in seconds. After hours of practice, Hedy pronounced my performance satisfactory.

"A lock that can't be opened with these requires a professional," she said.

My lie about being pregnant held several advantages. It gave me a believable excuse to avoid family activities, and a hiding place beneath my jeans. "Who would think it's anything but a baby bump? Or be bold enough to shove their hands there?" Hedy asked, when she made this suggestion.

After breakfast, while the others were busy, I determined to explore the house after checking the location of the housekeeper couple. The woman was cooking. I didn't see her husband but decided not to wait.

Margaret in Manhattan

I wondered who they really were. While a house this expensive required a year-round caretaker lest it be burglarized or worse, they seemed more than that. They were too watchful for ordinary servants and too sturdily built. They would look more natural in military garb, I thought.

I remembered what Vladimir once said: "It never pays to take someone wholly for what they seem even if that's the only thing you have to go on."

Chapter 125

Everyone has things in their life that they wish had never happened and can't forget. One of mine was my experience in Tokyo where I lay naked and tied to a table, awaiting torture and death. This tormenting memory will likely remain for the rest of my life.

Nightmares arising from it had forced me to consult a doctor in Berlin. Afterward, they had disappeared until the previous night. But this dream hadn't been as bad as in the past when my screams awoke the household. Now I just whimpered and, hearing this, Randy held me close.

He hadn't asked what troubled me. He understood that some questions were best left unasked. Ignorance isn't bliss but can sometimes allow you to sleep at night.

Did my nightmare predict disaster? I asked myself. That's impossible! I silently replied. Sigmund Freud, the father of psychoanalysis, had denied that dreams foretold the future. But, he added, they *can* suggest what is known to be true, like the danger that we faced.

I retrieved the pistol and Tubular Lock Pick from its pillow-shaped hiding place against my belly, placing them in my jacket pocket from which they could be more easily retrieved. Then I began exploring.

I didn't bother with the rooms that I had already seen: kitchen and library and dining room. Private activities wouldn't be conducted in public view. For the same reason, I ignored the second-floor which contained the bedrooms. Randy and I had seen them. They contained only beds and typical furnishings. But I hadn't been to the cellar and it was there that I began investigating.

Margaret in Manhattan

I tried to brush from my mind another thought: that in horror movies, the worst things happen in the cellar. But that's also where families watch TV and play, I told myself, as I approached the door. It was unlocked and a low-watt bulb dimly lit the stairway. I cautiously descended the stairs, after softly closing the door behind me.

Chapter 126

People who are engaged in illegal deeds want secrecy and isolation, a dark, furtive corner. They don't want to stand out, for which this house was ideal. It was in a rural area, surrounded by trees and having no close neighbors. Loud noises and even gunshots would be ignored. They would be considered hunting or target practice, gun ownership being widespread here unlike in New York City.

Such gloomy thoughts cluttered my mind as I descended the stairs, cursing myself for having watched popular thrillers. At the landing, I noted the surroundings before continuing.

To the right was the boiler room. To the left was a storage room filled with discarded furniture and crates. At the rear was a steel security door. The door was open and from just outside it came the sound of voices.

I couldn't initially make out the words but the tone was angry. The older, louder voices were those of a man and a woman. The younger male tone was hesitant but determined.

I hid behind the crates, hoping to see who was speaking and to hear what was being said but feared being discovered. I also feared becoming locked in the basement when they left.

Their conversation went on irregularly for a few minutes. When it seemed over, I cautiously left my hiding space and climbed the stairs. At the door, I turned for one final glance. Two men and a woman had left the room after shoving the youth inside and locking its door. They hadn't seen me.

I shoved my fist into my mouth to keep from crying out. Two of them were my targets. One was Borya's "person of interest." The other, a youth, was tall with red-hair and angular features. I had never seen him before but knew him instantly. He was the male form of me: Creighton, my twin brother, who I had vowed to bring home.

Chapter 127

People in a hopeless position sometimes try to shape reality with positive thoughts and that's what I tried to do. I told myself that things weren't so bad, that the American government backed me as did Borya who I trusted far more.

Moreover, who was there to fear? A few people and maybe others that I hadn't seen. In their eyes, Randy and I were just an airhead teenager and her clueless boyfriend. Two idiots who had allowed themselves to travel with strangers to an isolated location with phone service that varied with the weather.

The graying sky concerned me and I had checked a weather app before leaving Manhattan. A paralyzing snowstorm was forecast to move up the East Coast and we would withstand the worst of it that day.

Throughout lunch I smiled and made silly comments as my mind lay elsewhere. Having seen my brother–my image, my blood–I couldn't relax. His jailers' anger and the locked, steel cell made it obvious that his life was endangered–as was our mother's. I didn't know how long she would live, how long I had to bring Creighton home.

He would know what was being planned in this house, and what he had apparently refused to do. Tomorrow might be too late. My dinnertime remarks were even stupider than usual as I tried to decide when to return to the cellar.

Late that evening, as I lay on a settee in the living room, my decision became easier. With the arrival of the storm, the electricity had begun to fail, giving me the welcome darkness that I needed.

Margaret in Manhattan

I walked to my bedroom. There, once again, I moved the pistol and lock picks from my belly pouch to my pockets and checked the flashlight app on my fully-charged phone. Then I went to the cellar.

Chapter 128

Though still young, I had already learned that some people must do terrible things to survive. While walking toward the cellar, I wondered about Creighton's experiences. These thoughts slowed my steps and I forced them from my mind.

I met no one as the household lights flickered. Likely, everyone was sheltered in their room. I had left Randy sleeping to avoid his objections. If I'm successful, he will soon learn. And if I fail, he will soon learn this too, I thought.

I had heard voices while passing the boys' room and stood frozen, thinking up a plausible excuse to use. But I soon realized that they came from a video game being played far past their bedtime.

The rest of my journey went untroubled as I approached the cellar. I descended the stairs slowly using the flashlight app as illumination. The cellar's low-watt bulb wasn't working.

I paused at the locked steel door and listened. Hearing nothing, I cautiously inserted the electrical lock pick. It worked as intended, making only the slightest sound. I cautiously entered the room, holding the PSS silent pistol before me, ready for battle.

I shone my phone's flashlight over its interior. One corner contained a dresser and wooden chair. Another corner held a toilet and washstand. I focused on the third corner. There, lying on a bed, lay Creighton.

The mattress was thin and, despite the chill in the room, only a thin blanket covered him. There was a chain around his ankle, fastened to a metal eyelet on the bed with a padlock.

When I moved closer, he sprang awake and faced me. There were marks on his face from beatings.

He scowled as he stared at my face. I was a stranger yet in some way familiar too. When he spoke, it was as if he had been isolated for a long time and had to learn to speak anew. His gaze turned to the pistol in my hand.

"Who are you? Have you come to kill me?" he asked, in a hoarse whisper.

At first, choked with emotion, I was unable to speak. But moments later I spoke in a firm voice.

"I'm your sister. I've come to bring you home," I said.

Chapter 129

I opened the padlock with the lock pick and removed the chain encircling Creighton's ankle. Once freed, he stretched and lay back on the bed, seeming unable to speak.

My anxiety increased. I didn't know how long we would remain undiscovered or what to do next but he needed time to recover. When he seemed more relaxed, I began questioning him.

"How long have you been here?" I asked.

"I'm not sure, maybe a month. I lost track of time after the first few days." he said, with the hint of a shrug.

"Why are they keeping you here?" I asked.

"To punish me because I *lack obedience*."

"Who is doing this?" I asked.

"My parents. No, those who I had *believed* to be my parents, who I grew up," he said, hesitantly.

I thought for several seconds. His answers raised many questions but what do I need to know *now*? I asked myself.

"What did you refuse to do?" I asked.

"A test."

"What kind of a test?" I asked.

"They wanted me to pick-up a girl at the bus station and bring her here. A run-a-way, someone who could disappear without questions being asked locally," Creighton said.

"Why did they want her? Are they running a sex cult?" I asked.

"I wish," Creighton said, with the slightest hint of a smile.

He seemed to be regaining normal feelings and I didn't want to interrupt him. I waited, and the answer came.

"They have a gas to test. They want to assure its killing power," he said, in a monotone.

The horror of what was said brought me back to my mission. Reuniting with my brother wasn't a national interest. Finding the "person of interest" and foiling mass murder were.

"Do you know where the gas is being produced or stored?" I asked.

"There's another wing to this house. Its entrance is behind what looks like a solid brick wall. The opening switch is behind the framed photo of West Point. It's meant as a joke since that's the target.

"The plan is to paralyze America by killing its military elite. The gas lingers so removing it won't be quick or easy," Creighton said.

Then he seemed to remember where we were.

"There's more than just you here, isn't there?" he asked, hopefully.

Chapter 130

Though Creighton's question—if I was alone—was *the* question considering our peril, others swirled through my mind. What had he experienced during his nineteen years, and how had he discovered his identity? Then I caught myself. These answers must come later, achieving safety came first.

"How many are with you?" he repeated.

"There's just me. Our plan didn't go as intended," I said, calmly.

Creighton's eyes sunk back into his head.

"*You* don't know who you're dealing with," he said, despairingly.

His hopeless tone brought me fully back to myself and aroused my rage.

"*They* don't know who they're dealing with. Let's get you out of here," I said forcefully.

"Can you walk?" I asked, grasping his arm.

"Yes. I forced myself to exercise. I'm OK that way," he replied.

Afterward, I realized that I hadn't been thinking clearly. It would have been smartest to leave Creighton as I found him. Then, to return to my room and seek reinforcements. One underpowered pistol against an unknown number of enemy wasn't good odds.

But I couldn't leave him even if this would have been the logical thing to do. He had suffered too long. What kind of person would I be if I allowed his torment to continue?

Moreover, could he survive abandonment psychologically when freedom had seemed so near? I shrugged to myself as we left the room, resolved to fail or to succeed.

I would hide Creighton in my room though this could be only a temporary measure. Once his escape was discovered, an exhaustive search of the house was inevitable and the gloves would come off. The only suspects would be the clueless teenagers, who might not be so dumb after all. Only one small pistol, I thought again.

Chapter 131

I led the way with my pistol. From his cell, along the basement corridor, and up the stairs. We both wore sneakers and his steps were as silent as mine. Before opening the door to my room, I held my finger over my lips, not wanting him to cry out when he saw Randy's sleeping figure.

I tugged Randy's shoulder. He awoke dreamily and reached for me before seeing Creighton. I covered his mouth with my hand.

"He's my brother. He was being held prisoner and we must flee," I whispered.

Despite being a genius, Randy isn't the quickest thinker about practical matters but he didn't argue. He simply nodded and dressed quickly.

"Dress warmly," I cautioned.

I looked around for cold-weather clothes that Creighton could wear. He is two inches taller than Randy but Randy's clothes fit him. The predicted blizzard had arrived and snow covered the landscape. It would be no good to escape the house's danger and die from frostbite.

I heard video game play as we passed the boys' bedroom and this normal sound calmed me. We are just leaving the house to go for a walk, I told myself. One step after another, along the corridor, down the stairway to the outer door.

An unwelcome thought suddenly invaded my mind: was there a locked deadbolt on the front door? I didn't remember and had left my lock pick kit in the bedroom. Anxiety again overtook me.

Margaret in Manhattan

But this worry was unfounded. The front door had an ordinary lock that opened with a simple turn. I checked to see that Randy and Creighton were close behind and they were. A heavy wind and blast of snow entered the hallway when I opened the door. It staggered me and I nearly lost my footing on the slippery tile.

I turned to reassure myself that the others were OK but they obviously weren't. Both stood as if they were paralyzed before falling slowly to the ground. Then the same happened to me.

Chapter 132

Were I thinking clearly, I would have been less frightened. I had been Tasered in London three years before and survived. But when it happens, your thinking goes out the window.

You've probably read that Tasers give off fifty-thousand volts but that's not what enters the body. What penetrates is much less but still enough to do its job which is to disrupt a body's ecosystem. It's a whole-body experience.

What is felt is not the Taser's barb pricks but every muscle in your body contracting and twitching at once. Unless you're hopped up on drugs, you *will* fall.

I went down and didn't try to get up. After being Tasered, even the toughest victim feels dizzy and disoriented. They would beg not to have the experience repeated. But even if we tried, fighting back wouldn't have succeeded.

Four muscled, armed men pulled us to our feet and propelled us toward a locked room at the back of the house. In the still erratic house lighting, it looked like a storeroom filled with castaways: packing cases, a beat-up couch and recliner, folded heavy blankets, and an ironing board. Nothing that could be used as a weapon, I noted.

Randy and I fell upon the couch and Creighton took the recliner.

"What's Plan B?" Randy asked.

"It hasn't been written. When I found Creighton, Plan A went even more wrong," I said.

Creighton looked toward us.

"I'm glad you came to save me but you might have taken an earlier bus," he said.

He seemed to have my quirky senses of humor.

"Things aren't that bad if we can still joke," Randy said.

"People sometimes joke to lessen the pain of a terrible situation," I said.

"Their plan has probably changed too," Creighton said.

"How so?" I asked.

"Why risk kidnapping someone to test the gas when they already have three people to get rid of," he replied.

What Creighton said made sense. We had to die so why not benefit from our deaths?

I shrugged, closed my eyes, and prayed.

Chapter 133

Snow filled the sky. Dawn was several hours away. It would soon be time for breakfast though we didn't expect any. Food wouldn't be wasted on those who would shortly be dead.

The worst thing would be to lose hope, I reminded myself. I tried being hopeful but didn't succeed. I couldn't help thinking how things might have been different.

Randy managed to doze and, upon awakening, he looked relaxed.

"I dreamt about angels. They came to our rescue and saved us," he said.

This surprised me since Randy and his family aren't religious and he had never spoken of a dream containing religious symbolism.

I smiled and hugged him but said nothing, feeling too depressed.

"I will be succeeding at one thing," he said.

"What's that?" I asked.

"To remain with you until my death," Randy said.

I hugged him tightly. Tears filled my eyes and I was unable to speak.

"There was something odd in the dream," Randy said, after a pause.

"What was that?" I asked.

"The leading angel had a broken wing," he said.

"A broken wing," I repeated, slowly.

The word "broken" had struck me as being significant though I couldn't imagine how. Then I suddenly did.

I prayed, and squeezed the fleshy part of my thumb until a small red dot appeared. Then I held Randy tighter.

"*What*?" he asked.

"I've just made a Hail Mary."

"What's that?" Randy asked.

He's not interested in sports.

"What a desperate football player does when his team's position seems hopeless. He prays before his final throw, having only one chance in a million to succeed," I explained.

Randy looked puzzled but said nothing. I pulled off my jeans and panties, wriggled atop him, and we comforted each other in the only way left, clinging to life.

Chapter 134

"What time is it?" Randy asked, in a whisper, conscious that Creighton dozed nearby.

"They took my watch too," I replied.

Randy rose from the couch and pulled on his pants. I slipped on my panties and jeans. He went to the window and stared into the snowy mist.

"That's funny."

"What is?" I asked.

"There are flashes, like the angels in my dream. They're swooping toward the house," Randy said.

I walked to the window and stared out.

"They're skiers," I said.

A memory came to mind, a story that Vladimir had told me about the Second World War. In its early days when defeat seemed certain, fresh Russian ski troops had pounced upon and defeated the Nazi invaders. But curiosity replaced hope as I reminded myself that this is now in America.

Loud noises followed, from explosions and pistol and automatic weapons being fired. I pulled Randy back from the window as it shattered and a small black object hurtled in. It's a sting grenade, the non-paralyzed part of my mind told me.

I pushed Randy down upon the sofa and covered us with a blanket while yelling to Creighton to do the same. Then came an ear-shattering sound followed by hard shrapnel pellets smashing into the blanket. Some of them hit my exposed hands and legs and pain shot threw me.

Disoriented and terrified, I scrambled to my feet. The floor was littered with what seemed like small marbles. Then the door burst open and three men entered the room. Two wore face shields and carried sub-machine guns. The third was unshielded and held a pistol. It was he who spoke.

"Are you all right? Who is this man?" Borya asked, as his gaze and pistol turned upon Creighton.

Deadly accidents happen in such circumstances. I spoke quickly using a name that he would instantly respond to.

"He's Vladimir's son, my twin brother."

Borya's pistol was returned to its holster. He embraced Creighton in a bear hug and Creighton didn't resist. A friendly hug beats a leveled pistol any day.

"Vladimir's son, my dear boy," Borya said, with deep feeling.

The Russians are an emotional people.

Though Borya's nickname is *Lucifer*, the Devil, that morning he was our Angel.

Chapter 135

We dressed quickly and left the building. The snowfall had tapered into showers as four SUVs and a small truck awaited our departure. Randy, Creighton, the boys, and I were bundled into one car. The boys sat beside Randy. He was now their only friend in their changed life.

We didn't know how many others in the house remained alive. I didn't learn what happened until later.

Later, was at a rented house several miles down the road. There, I spoke with Borya while Randy comforted the children by, as you might expect, playing video games. Much of their popularity comes from its ability to reduce stress.

The Hail Mary pass had worked. Before leaving Manhattan, Borya had arranged for a powerful microchip, the size of a grain of rice, to be inserted into the fleshy part of my thumb.

A simpler model has been used with workers at Stockholm's Epicenter/co-working space since 2015. With it, people do things that they usually use credit cards and keys for. Using my implanted microchip, Borya had been able to track my location.

His agent had been watching the house through binoculars since we arrived. When I broke the chip and thus contact with them, they correctly interpreted this as my signal that something was wrong. More agents were brought in to storm the house.

These men were Russian ski troops. They had entered the country legally, supposedly to compete in a ski competition which they afterward rejoined.

Margaret in Manhattan

After the assault, videos were taken of the house and its chemical weapons equipment before their removal or destruction by explosives. The "person of interest," Creighton's parents, and the boys' parents were cuffed and driven to nearby Kingston harbor. There, they were placed on a speedboat which carried them to a Russian freighter docked in international waters. Their fate was secure and America was safe.

Had West Point been attacked and America learned that a Russian scientist was involved, war between the two nations could have resulted.

But the widely-published explanations were vastly different. They stated that the house had been a manufacturing facility for illegal drugs. It had been stormed by a rival gang and bullet-ridden bodies were found in the wreckage.

More money was needed to combat drug addiction and crime, the county's District Attorney railed, and that was it. And of Creighton and his parents, the boys and their parents, and "the person of interest"? They never existed.

Of course, what really happened couldn't be kept from the government agencies–who were manic! Russian agents operating in America? Despite the fortunate outcome, a furious Congress might impeach the President if they learned.

High-level conferences followed during which a fictional narrative was constructed. The men who stormed the house became Drug Enforcement Agency agents acting on information from the FBI and CIA. Though deserving recognition, they could not be identified because of their continuing undercover activities. Instead, promotions were given to agency officials and everyone was happy.

Margaret in Manhattan

Vladimir's comment on what newspapers called "The New York Drug Battle" became widely shared by those who knew what really happened: "A good plan violently executed is better than a great plan later. Truth can be as terrible as death but harder to find," he had said.

Chapter 136

The story that the boys were told was also fictional. When a drug-crazed gang invaded their home, their parents had battled heroically to save them at the cost of their lives. The holes in this story weren't noticed.

The boys already knew that they were adopted. Several days later they were told that their biological mother, Olga, had been found. She had placed them for adoption from fear that, because of her youth, she wouldn't be a good-enough mother. All their parents had loved them, they were assured.

The tale was good one. While the boys were stoic, Olga was tearful. They walked off arm-in-arm to create a new life in Berlin. The boys' American passports were found and they would receive German passports once DNA evidence was submitted.

Another happy outcome was my reunion with Creighton. This didn't go as well since Creighton hadn't known that he was adopted. The shock of learning this added to the stress from his recent imprisonment, anticipated murder, and discovery that he had a twin sister.

Much like a soldier who had endured too many battles, he became moody with long periods of silence and nightmares.

I developed similar behaviors after my rescue from kidnap three years earlier. Psychotherapy had helped me, and was recommended for Creighton.

Doctor Kandey suggested that Creighton spend a few weeks at a local psychiatric hospital where he could be regularly visited by members of his new family. The hospital in Greenwich was ideal since it is owned and managed by our mother, Lena.

Creighton's room had a disciplined color scheme of beige, blue-green, and brown. The mural of an 18th century garden scene reinforced the relaxed, country look while the light-colored upholstery and rug made the room seem modern.

Because of his fragility, Creighton hadn't been told of our mother's mortal illness. I had intended to meet with him alone for our first real talk but was advised not to.

Chapter 137

Despite their deceit, the Young parents had been *real* parents to their sons. They encouraged their spontaneity and normal school experience, not having yet begun their training as sleeper agents. But Creighton's life had been different.

He had been home-tutored and discouraged from making friends. His life had been controlled–until the recent weeks when he rebelled. He was not a killer and would not be made into one. Now, separated from his familiar surroundings, he felt alone and adrift.

Creighton didn't understand the concept of friendship and lacked the capacity to trust. He had never experienced warmth from another person. He was like a newborn, or an alien from another planet.

Doctor Crowe, Creighton's therapist, suggested that I not initially speak with Creighton alone. That he might experience this as too frightening and withdrew even more. Doctor Crowe advised me to bring friends, for Creighton's comfort and to begin his education of what friendship was. So I invited Erika, and her fiancée, Clarence, to our meeting.

It was a good choice for both had experienced suffering. Erika's mother and sister were murdered when she was a child and Clarence had dropped out of high school rather than endure bullying. With professional help and each other, they had made new, better lives.

The hospital was an "open" setting with patients being free to leave the grounds. I had thought of our seeing a movie but only thrillers were playing locally. Considering recent events, none would have been a good choice. We settled for lounging over snacks in the nearly empty cafeteria, on one of the plush sofas that bordered the walls.

The room didn't resemble a hospital. None of the professional staff wore uniforms and the patients' dress ranged from Greenwich casual to Manhattan elegant. I nibbled on my peach tart, Erika and Clarence ate their chocolate ice cream, and Creighton stared at his bottled water. My hope for pleasant conversation was being dashed.

Chapter 138

Women are usually better than men at making conversation so Erika and I took the lead. We chatted about high school memories and Greenwich events, hoping that the boys would join in.

Clarence did his best to broaden the dialog by revealing that he had been a high school drop-out. He became happy only after leaving school and "meeting Erika too," he added, with a smile that they shared.

Despite these efforts, Creighton remained unengaged with a bored look on his face. He removed a pad and pen from his jacket pocket and began scribbling. The small page was rapidly filling with math symbols. Erika and I stared at each other and waited. Clarence spoke before I could.

"You actually think that you can solve it?" he asked Creighton, with a look of surprise and admiration.

"I think so but aren't sure," Creighton replied.

These were his first words since the simple "hello" when we met.

"Please bring us into it," Erika requested, in an annoyed tone.

Clarence turned toward Creighton.

"Me or you?" he asked.

Creighton shrugged.

"Creighton is trying to solve one of the seven most difficult problems in mathematics," Clarence said.

Margaret in Manhattan

He waited for a moment before continuing, as if he had just dropped a bombshell, and pointed to the text as he spoke.

"The Clay Mathematics Institute has offered a one-million-dollar prize for their solutions but only one has been achieved, by the Russian mathematician Grigori Perelman in 2003.

"Creighton is working on the Birch and Swinnerton-Dyer conjecture. This describes the set of rational solutions to equations defining an elliptic curve. The speculation relates arithmetic data associated with an elliptic curve E over a number field K to the behavior of the Hasse-Weil L-function $L(E,s)$ of E at $s=1$.

"More precisely, it is estimated that the rank of the abelian group $E(K)$ of points of E is the order of the zero of $L(E,s)$ at $s=1$, and the first non-zero coefficient in the Taylor expansion of $L(E,s)$ at $s=1$ is given by more refined arithmetic data attacked to E over K."

"Have I got it right?" Clarence asked Creighton.

"I couldn't have explained it better," came the reply, with a grin.

Creighton's smile was his first expression of enjoyment that afternoon. I stared at Erika. It appeared that Clarence, who is a math and computer whiz, had found a new friend, and that Clarence might have found his first.

Chapter 139

Erika and I left the boys, who were chatting excitedly, a few minutes later. Their passion for math wasn't ours and they needed time to bond. We passed the recreation room and decided to hang out there.

The room had the usual huge TV screen that one finds in hospitals but also comfortable sofas and vending machines with free healthy snacks. We both chose yoghurt, I, the non-fat plain, and she, the non-fat vanilla. Then we sprawled on the sofa farthest from the patients.

"What do you think?" I asked Erika.

"Your brother is *very* good looking," she replied.

"I already knew that," I said.

"But he's also a bit weird, in a way that seems familiar but I can't place it."

"He's like Kimberly?" I suggested, having already thought this.

"Exactly," Erika agreed.

I had met Kimberly at Barnard, when we roomed at Brooks Hall down the corridor from each other. Her sorrows included the early deaths of her parents, becoming a mother following rape by her cousin, and being falsely accused of drug dealing and murder. After being cleared and released from jail, she and her daughter had moved to Greenwich.

Kimberly was odd when we first met. If asked something, she would reply with what was on her mind rather than answer the question. Like if I asked how a teacher was, she might tell me about Brazil, where she came from, or whatever else she had been thinking about.

I later decided that she might suffer from something like Asperger's Disorder since though being talented mathematically and with computers, she had grave social handicaps.

Her odd behavior had made it hard for her to socialize and I was her only friend at college. But this also helped me since she was a skillful math tutor.

Kimberly worked at the computer startup that Clarence's parents and Erika's billionaire father had established. Not that she needs the money. Her father was a super-rich industrialist and, after his death, she became the sixth richest woman in America. That was two years before. Her uncle handles her fortune and she only occasionally checks her status.

"Maybe we can fix the two of them up," Erika suggested, with a smile.

I just stared at her. It was *my brother* that she was joking about.

Chapter 140

We lounged in the recreation room for another half-hour, not saying much of anything, before rejoining the boys. After Erika left the hospital with Clarence, I walked with Creighton back to his room. He was now more relaxed and I risked a personal question.

"Have you considered what you'll do when you leave here?" I asked, being reluctant to use the word "hospital.".

"A little," he replied.

I waited silently and his answer finally came as we sat in his room. Like with Kimberly, talking wasn't easy for Creighton. Erika's lighthearted idea, that we should "fix them up," now seemed sensible.

But only for *friendship* and not romance, since that was far from what Creighton could tolerate. With someone having similar interests and difficulties though Kimberly's social skills had greatly improved. I hoped the same for Creighton.

"I want to be in a class with other students, and get a job. I read online that there's a huge demand for cryptography workers and I like solving puzzles," Creighton said.

"Those are *wonderful* ideas. Randy studies computer science at Yale and he could talk with his professor about you attending classes. They have a few home-schooled students and Randy said they're among the best. During your free time you could work with Clarence at his parents' startup. They would love to have you," I said.

I feared that I had said too much, that Creighton might consider me bossy and trying to control his life. But this didn't happen for he smiled appreciatively and appeared grateful.

Our shared conditions of being twins and adopted had already created a level of trust.

It was unavoidable that Creighton would meet Kimberly but this was something that I didn't say. I had noticed that Creighton ignored the interested stares that women gave him as we strolled through the hospital and around town. Apparently, sex wasn't something that he was ready for despite his grownup appearance. I had been a late-bloomer too.

Not wanting my presence to become a strain, I risked kissing Creighton on the cheek and left. There were math books on his desk and I sensed, from his glances, that he was impatient to return to them. He had told me that he taught himself calculus when he was nine. People like that are different from you and me.

Chapter 141

Since learning of her diagnosis, Lena had been working mostly from home. But this had worked well since she was a good manager and had hired efficient employees. The hospital didn't need her presence as much as when she bought it. It had become profitable and she gave frequent talks, having become a management leader.

Creighton hadn't yet been told that Lena was our mother. This would be another shock to endure, when Doctor Crowe felt that he was ready. And it wouldn't be his only surprise.

He need also learn that Vladimir, who lived in Berlin, was his *possible* father, since it might also be Peter, who lived in London, and that Peter also considered me his daughter. These opportune lies had added up, creating the huge, seemingly insoluble problem that we confronted.

That Lena had simultaneous affairs with both men when she conceived was undeniable. What was also irrefutable was that one or both men could, biologically, be our father. So Creighton might be my brother or my step-brother.

The truth about me could have been discovered through DNA testing but, as the years passed, it became increasingly difficult for Lena to request this. Thus both Peter and Vladimir had continued relating to me as their daughter. I treated both as a father and their relationship was cordial. They co-managed the same company in different countries.

But with Creighton's arrival into our fold, decisions had to be made. What to tell everyone was the first thing that we discussed when I arrived at my mother's apartment later that afternoon. I saw no painless way of dealing with this issue. Nor, at first, had Lena.

But as some wit said, "Telling the truth is the best policy. I've tried everything else." That was Lena's decision too.

"It's time that all learned," she said.

Chapter 142

We were sitting in the living room of her three-bedroom apartment. Twice widowed, she had done "the house thing" during her marriages, thereby losing her nesting instinct. Despite this, the room's old-fashioned décor had a homey quality with its comfortable furniture and thick rug.

When I arrived, she asked what parents usually do: if I was hungry. I settled for juice and she poured coffee for herself. Mormons typically don't drink coffee but Lena's faith had long since lapsed.

Her first husband was Evangelical Protestant. Her second husband was Jewish and Lena now belonged to the local synagogue. I thought again of what Mother Marie, an *iyalawo* (Santeria priestess), had said, "The Gods are not jealous."

I had remained silent so Lena repeated what she said: "It's time that all learned."

"It's amazing they haven't questioned this yet, that Vladimir and Peter could both believe I am their child," I said.

"They're old school and very private. Discussing their sexual experiences is unthinkable to one of their generation," Lena said.

"When will you tell them?" I asked.

"Tomorrow, after a good night's sleep. Creighton is being discharged from the hospital next week and I want him to meet them before..."

Lena didn't have to spell it out. *Before I die*, she had been about to say. My thinking turned to her health.

"How are you?" I asked.

"Surprisingly, I feel better. Not completely myself, but *better*. But this doesn't mean anything. There can be remissions with all medical problems."

"What's your current treatment?" I asked.

"There isn't any. The oncologist became sick and retired and his replacement hasn't arrived. I asked for a copy of my medical record to get a second opinion but it hasn't come yet and I haven't called. I've been dallying, like most people who fear the worst."

"*B'ao ku ishe o tan*," I said, softly, almost as a blessing.

"*What*?" Lena asked.

"It's an ancient African proverb meaning, 'when there is life, there is still hope,'" I said.

I didn't add that it came from the Santeria religion. My practicing both it and the Mormon faith was something that I hadn't shared with Lena. Some matters are best kept from one's parents.

Chapter 143

Both Vladimir and Peter welcomed our prospective visit and hungered to meet Creighton, their son. I didn't even try to predict their reactions upon learning the truth about his parentage, or Creighton's behavior either.

Not only had he lost his adoptive parents, lousy as they were, he had gained a new mother and either an English or a Russian father. No one, not even a genius, could accept these changes calmly.

Another upheaval was his new identity. Fearing that his life might be endangered, Lee had arranged for him to be placed in the Witness Protection Program and given a new identity. Using Lena's surname by marriage, Creighton was provided a Social Security number and Greenwich High School diploma in that name. Thus did I and my brother come to graduate in the same class.

I spent much time with Creighton before leaving for Europe, doing what teenagers do. We hung out at the Greenwich Library, where he got his first library card. We took the town ferry and walked along the Greenwich beach. We went to Greenwich High School to familiarize him with it if he were ever questioned.

I even introduced him to my favorite English teacher, Mrs. Carrobin, who welcomed our visit without being told its purpose. Then I took him to the Connecticut Department of Motor Vehicles to apply for his Learner's Permit. Few Greenwich teenagers lack a Driver's License.

Besides Randy, others accompanied us on these jaunts: Clarence, Erika, and her cousin, Maureen. All were easy-going and provided Creighton with what he needed: undemanding friendly warmth without the pressure of inquisitive questions.

The days passed quickly. Our flight to London would leave on Thursday morning and Creighton's first meeting with Lena, in Doctor Crowe's office, had been scheduled for the previous Monday.

Chapter 144

Doctor Crowe's office was like all the therapists' offices that I'd seen. It had a desk and office chair, a sofa, and two club chairs, one of which he sat on. There was also an old-fashioned analyst's couch that I wondered if anyone used nowadays. It might have been kept from custom or to indicate his rank in the profession, that he was a trained psychoanalyst.

Creighton, me, and our mother sat on the sofa. Doctor Crowe sat opposite us and began the meeting with a joke.

"Things can't be too bad if you're all sitting on the same sofa," he said, with a smile.

Then, after Lena revealed to Creighton that she was his biological mother, Doctor Crowe spoke to him.

"Your mother has something else to tell you," he said, in a somber tone.

Lena looked from Creighton to me before speaking.

"You've both led complicated lives, not knowing your origin until recently. Margaret didn't know that I was her biological mother until several years ago and you just learned this. The identity of your father is more complicated," Lena said.

She paused to sip from the coffee that she had brought with her.

"When I conceived, I was having simultaneous affairs with two men: Peter, who lived in London, and Vladimir, who lived in Berlin. My business in Belgium had involved me with both.

"They're exceptional men and you would be proud to have either as your father. Peter or Vladimir could have fathered you both or maybe just one of you, which would make you half-siblings.

"Who it is could have been discovered with DNA testing but this wasn't done and doing it now wouldn't make sense. I'm wealthy enough to help with each of your careers and expect you both to do brilliantly.

"Vladimir and Peter are old school so whatever questions they had likely remained unspoken. Both relate to Margaret as their daughter. They would regard you, Creighton, as their son. But life is finite and the matter has become thorny. I've told them the truth and, next week, you're traveling to Europe to meet them."

Lena's gaze had shifted from Creighton to me as she spoke. Guilt seemed to course through her and unspoken pain is crueler. When she finished speaking, she stared at Creighton. Though he was fragile and about whom we worried, the logic of his question and its tone reassured us.

"My education has admittedly been limited but is it really possible for twins to have *two* fathers?" he asked, calmly.

Chapter 145

Doctor Crowe smiled and leaned back in his chair.

"That's a *very* good question," he said.

Doctor Crowe then began a lengthy technical explanation, which was probably more than Creighton wanted.

"Despite popular notions, the conception of twins isn't simple. Normal males have an X and a Y chromosome while females have two X chromosomes. Identical twins are usually the same gender, either boys or girls. But, rarely, they begin as males, sharing XY chromosomes which are needed to create male reproductive systems and traits, before changing to become a male and a female.

"This happens when one-half of the split fertilized egg loses a copy of its genetically encoded Y chromosome early in pregnancy. The resultant babies then include one defined male with the proper chromosomes and a female who carries what is termed XO chromosomes. They have only one X chromosome rather than two, which is used by biologists to classify females. Because of this, the female lacks the hormones needed to grow properly and to reproduce. Medically, this is called Turner Syndrome.

"Nonidentical, or fraternal, twins occur when a woman produces *two* separate eggs that are then fertilized by *two* different sperm cells. These twins sometimes look alike but have separate genetic identities. They are like children of the same parents that were born during different pregnancies.

"Fraternal twins form when two eggs release during the same ovulation. Sometimes, the eggs release simultaneously.

In other cases, the ovaries initially release one egg which, after fertilization, moves to the uterus to attach.

"The ovaries then release a second egg. This becomes fertilized by a later act of sexual intercourse which can be with a different man's sperm. One to two percent of fraternal twins have different fathers, as may or may not have happened with you and your sister. Have I answered your question, Creighton?"

"*Eminently.* The issue seems straight-forward to me. Margaret and I are fine. How Peter and Vladimir react to us depends on them," Creighton said.

We all smiled as the tension in the room lifted.

"I couldn't have said it better," Doctor Crowe said, sympathetically.

Chapter 146

Creighton's behavior improved steadily over the following week. His mood swings and silences were fewer and he participated more in his group therapy. He also began reading the *Greenwich Times* which is delivered daily to the Hospital. He wanted to learn about his new community, he said.

I learned of these changes from him. It wouldn't have been proper for Doctor Crowe or Lena to tell me, even as Creighton and I grew closer as siblings do.

I wanted to introduce him to my adoptive family and they wanted this too. Lena suggested that I take it slow.

"Change is best taken in small steps. When you return from Europe is time enough," she said.

But Creighton's curiosity wouldn't wait. He pressed me with questions about Peter and Vladimir, and about London and Berlin too. He had traveled little and hungered to know the world and his ancestry.

What I told him wasn't everything. It wasn't a fairy tale but not exactly the truth either.

I said that Peter is a former spy and national British hero, and that Vladimir had been a Russian general. Though historically on opposing national sides, they now managed, along with a retired Central Intelligence Agency official, an international security company that served wealthy individuals and Western nations.

I left out some details: Peter's adventures; the murder of Vladimir's daughter in a Moscow terrorist attack; our Uncle Borya's nickname of *Lucifer*, the Devil; and that Lena's first job, after being expelled from school for selling marijuana and running away from home, was office work at an escort service.

About myself, I shared only that I was a Barnard student and expected to marry Randy. Nothing of the events in Tokyo and London and Berlin. Creighton wasn't yet healthy enough to hear those.

Chapter 147

The days flew by and there were many things that we had to do before leaving. Creighton didn't have acceptable clothes for travel so Erika and I took him shopping. She had long shopped for her father and I shop for Randy since both men hate it.

We went to Richards which is a Greenwich institution. When seeking the best selection of fine clothes under one roof, you can't do better locally than here.

Their prices are high but money wasn't an issue. Lena had lent me her Richard's charge card and I planned to apply for one that day.

Richard's is in the center of town and walking in the neighborhood is always a pleasure. Another advantage is that the store has its own parking lot. Finding street parking in Greenwich is always a problem.

Lee worried about Creighton's safety. Though some of the sleeper agents had been arrested, it wasn't known how large the ring was or of their thirst for vengeance.

As the daughter of a billionaire, fear of kidnap was never far from Erika's mind. Now, *two* of her bodyguards accompanied us as we drove to Richards in one of her family's armored SUVs. A compartment between the front seats holds short-barreled submachine guns.

Creighton's real danger that day was from the girls that his good looks attracted. Their inviting eyes followed him as we strolled through the store.

Margaret in Manhattan

As he gazed in wonderment at the racks, his glittering smile occasionally paralyzed the Personal Shopper that had been assigned him.

She ("Call me Christy") took his arm as they walked through the store with Erika, me, and the bodyguards trailing along. I turned toward Erika and smiled, we both having the same thought: Creighton would need protecting from women.

Chapter 148

After selecting clothes with Creighton (suits, sport jacket, shirts, slacks, jeans, underwear, shoes, and socks), Christy, his Personal Shopper, pronounced him "fitted" and we left the store. She did everything except hug him as we left. I didn't consider her excitement related to the fifty-nine-hundred-dollar charge. My brother is *that* good-looking.

After leaving Richards, I suggested that we drive around Greenwich to acquaint Creighton with his new home town and no one disagreed. We drove slowly along Greenwich Avenue, first south toward the train station and then turning north, stopping at the Library.

Creighton's personality is like Randy's in at least one respect: he lets others plan activities for him. Maybe because geniuses are most engaged inwardly.

Despite our chatter about the charms of Greenwich, Creighton seemed most comfortable at the Library. He wandered off with one of Erika's bodyguards as she and I gossiped in Elton's Café, the snack shop on the Library's lower level.

"It's frightening!" erupted a woman at a neighboring table.

When we looked toward her, she silently held up the *Greenwich Times'* front page. Its headline read, "Police Warn of Serial Rapist. Survivor to Speak at Community Meeting Tonight." Erika turned toward me.

"I'm going. Come with me," she said.

It was more a demand than a request but I nodded agreement. I didn't want to go but felt that I had no choice.

Years before, after her mother and sister were raped and murdered, Erika had considered suicide. She survived thanks to her lengthy therapy and support from her father and friends.

I doubted that the lecture would tell us safety precautions we didn't already know but understood why Erika had to attend. Some people must do terrible things to survive.

Chapter 149

Creighton had changed into his new clothes while at Richards.

"He looks like money," Erika said, approvingly.

"Wife bait," I said.

'You're too young to be so cynical. Women need security, for their babies," Erika said.

I didn't reply. Considering what Erika had experienced in her life, if anyone had a right to be cynical, she did. I was glad that she had regained her sunny mood.

While leaving the Library, Creighton spied a poster on the wall. It advertised the community meeting and he read it slowly.

"Are you two going?" he asked.

"Yes," Erika replied.

"I'll go too," he said.

I dodged, feeling that hearing a painful story wasn't advisable for him.

"Would the hospital let you go?" I asked.

"I no longer need their permission. I'm in the discharge unit, for patients who are soon leaving. It's like being on probation, you might say."

I didn't like the expression but saw his point. There was no tactful way for me to dissuade him. I was his sister and not his mother, or as much of a parent as one can be to a nineteen-year-old. I nodded acceptance and looked at Erika.

Margaret in Manhattan

"The meeting is at seventy-thirty. I'll pick *you* up at seven and then *you*," Erika said, nodding from Creighton toward me.

Suburban lectures aren't usually well attended no matter how good they are. Maybe because commuting places too great demands on family life for other intrusions or just their inconvenient time. The evening working hours of librarians tends to compete with dinner time.

But this meeting was packed. Fear motivates and women have few greater fears than of a serial rapist particularly since they rarely stop there. The rage that arouses rape often ends with murder.

Another surprise that night was the presence of many men. While most seemed part of a couple, I recognized several out-of-uniform police officers in the audience.

Sergeant Alamo smiled at me. He was close friends with my parents and had babysat me and my sisters. He stared at Creighton, our resemblance being distinctive. I made a mental note to introduce them later just as the moderator rapped his gavel to silence the room.

Chapter 150

The moderator was Police Chief Fellsen who I had previously met. He is huge: six-foot-four inches and two-hundred-forty pounds, with a massive chest and arms that had bench-pressed four-hundred-fifty pounds until he injured a shoulder.

He and my father had spoken at a fund-raiser for the Police Foundation which financially assists the families of fallen officers. I remembered the Chief's warm smile from that event. That evening he was grim as he looked about the room before speaking.

"We are here to honor Lydia, and to inform. To applaud a brave woman who survived, and holding the hope that others won't share her experience.

"Because police officers cannot be everywhere, you must do your part. In the handout are safety precautions that all should follow. Locking doors and windows and cars, having proper lighting and alarms and, if you possess a weapon, gaining the needed training.

"But most of all, to react instantly when you sense that something is not quite right. Safety, not the fear of being impolite or appearing silly, must be your priority. Each of our minds has a reptilian element, a survival instinct that has been present since humanity began. Pay attention to its warnings!

"Characteristic of Lydia's bravery is her insistence on being publicly identified. This happened once before, at her husband's funeral. He was slain while working as a New York City police officer. Afterward, she left Brooklyn and moved to Greenwich which she considered safer."

A gasp went through the audience. Chief Fellsen waited for silence before continuing.

"Lydia's experience emphasizes the evil that we must defeat. Her story will not be easy to tell, or to hear. But it may bring us closer to achieving justice for she and the other violated women.

"We only recently learned that a serial rapist stalks our area: in Byram, and in Stamford, and now in Greenwich. Why didn't we realize this sooner? Because it takes time to become aware of a criminal's modus operandi, and particularly when the crimes occur in different legal jurisdictions.

"All stranger rapists are serial rapists: it just depends on how soon you catch them in their succession of crimes.

"Lydia's information provided us with a key since even during her frightening moments she sought identifying facts about her attacker. Though this can't be revealed, it will eventually end his reign of terror."

Chief Fellsen turned to the slim brunette seated at his right.

"Lydia," he said softly, and she rose.

Chapter 151

Lydia was tall with brown hair down to her shoulders. She was modestly dressed in a dark blue suit and white blouse. Her maroon scarf seemed out-of-place and I wondered if it concealed bruises. She looked over the audience and then down at her notes before placing them aside.

"I'm no hero. I'm just a survivor and am here to tell you my story. My mistake led me to this platform, a place that I hope you can avoid," Lydia said, in a firm voice.

I looked around the audience. Her words had caught everyone's attention.

"My mistake was believing in absolute safety. I now realize this doesn't exist, not even in Greenwich. We must each do our part, as Chief Fellsen said.

"The night of the attack, I had locked the doors but neglected my daughter's window. I have two children: a seven-year-old girl and a four-year-old boy. Both were sleeping when the rapist pulled off the screen and pried open the window into her room. I was sleeping in my room.

"I first experienced him as a voice. Then as a hand covering my mouth and a pistol thrust into my face.

"Lydia, do what I say and your kids won't be hurt. Don't look at me," he murmured softly.

"I nodded that I understood and felt like vomiting."

"Take off your clothes!" he ordered.

"I shivered as I stripped. I felt that I had just minutes to live and thought of my children."

"What have you done to my children?" I whispered.

"Nothing, and they won't be harmed if you do as I say. Don't look at me!" he ordered.

"He pulled down his pants and forced his way into my mouth and then between my legs. I felt him ejaculate and wanted to kill him but was too afraid to move.

"When he was finished, he said, 'OK, you can get dressed but stay in bed and don't move.' I heard him walk from room to room, taking his time. A storm window rattled and he ran back into my room, thinking that I was making my escape. 'I said don't move,' he said, and grabbed my throat. I said, in a panicked voice, 'It wasn't me. I didn't move. I didn't!'

"Then he rummaged through the drawers, looking for cash and valuables. There wasn't much to steal: two phones, an iPad, a little over two-hundred dollars, my wedding and engagement rings, a gold necklace. He put everything into a pillow case before raping me orally and vaginally again.

"Then he dragged me to the living room and ordered me to put my hand on the window. 'I'm leaving and if I don't see your hand there, I'm coming back to kill you and your kids. Don't call the cops! I know every car in this neighborhood and if I see a strange one, I'll be back and first your kids will get it and then you.'"

Lydia paused to sip water before continuing.

Chapter 152

There were murmurings in the audience as Lydia resumed speaking. But now there was no need for Chief Fellsen to rap the gavel for silence. The room fell silent as soon as she put down her bottle of water.

"After standing with my hand against the window for a minute, I went to the phone and called the police. Then I climbed to the attic, found my late husband's shotgun, and loaded it. He had taught me to shoot skeet.

"After gathering my children, we waited for the police in the living room. When my daughter asked about the gun, I said that there had been a burglary and the police were coming but that we were safe. She accepted this explanation as a normal occurrence.

"The police took me to the hospital where I told the nurse what happened. 'Did you rinse your mouth or shower?' she asked. 'I rinsed my mouth,' I replied. 'That destroyed the evidence. You should have spit the semen into a cup or onto the bed,' she said, disapprovingly. 'Not when the rapist was holding a gun to my face,' I said.

"The nurse cut specimens of my hair and pubic hair for the rape kit and had me urinate into a cup. She ran ultraviolet light over my mouth and body, saying that semen shone in this light. When I left the hospital, I felt changed from a person to an object of investigation.

"I slept with my children that night but couldn't sleep, even with the shotgun on the floor. When I closed my eyes, I saw the rapist's body against mine.

"For weeks thereafter I couldn't strip naked to take a shower. I hated the thought of being naked and showered in a swimsuit. I jumped at every sound and avoided going out to not see people.

"I still feel fear and rage. I was told this is what happens after being violated no matter whether the crime is assault or burglary. That's my story."

Chief Fellsen rose.

"Lydia has agreed to answer questions," he said.

Chapter 153

At first no one in the audience moved. Perhaps fearing, like me, that questions would increase Lydia's pain. Slowly, hands rose and Chief Fellsen called upon them.

"How are you doing now?" an older, white-haired woman asked.

It was several moments before Lydia answered.

"I'm definitely better but sense that I won't feel safe until he's caught though absolute safety isn't possible. Right afterward I had a hard time concentrating even in ordinary conversations. And I wouldn't use the word 'rape.' Instead, I spoke of the *event* or *incident*.

"When I went outside, my eyes swiveled like a security camera, checking each man that passed. My presence here and speaking openly shows you how far I've come."

"What keeps you going?" asked a man in his twenties.

Lydia answered this question with greater confidence.

"My children. Young kids take all your time, and I can't let them see me afraid. I don't want them growing up afraid. My husband wouldn't have wanted it either."

"Just one more question before going downstairs to Elton's Café for refreshments. Lydia will join us until the Library closes at nine," Chief Fellsen said.

He called on a petite blond-haired woman.

"How has your experience most changed you, for the worse and the better?" she asked.

I considered this an excellent question.

Lydia paused before answering.

"My initial reaction to a stranger is no longer trust. Though I'm not sure whether you would consider this a benefit or a loss. I'm more cautious, and teach this to my children though recognizing that my concern sometimes borders on paranoia.

"I've begun seeing a therapist. I had a difficult childhood and this would have been a good decision years ago. It's making me a better parent too."

Lydia ended her answer with a dramatic flourish. From her handbag, she drew a small pistol and held it in her palm.

"Now, I also carry a gun," she said.

Chapter 154

People began drifting out as 9PM approached. I wanted to leave too but Creighton stared at Lydia and lingered. I remained by his side, sensing that his question had a personal meaning. When only the Chief and Lydia remained, Creighton approached her.

"My question is a bit delicate," he said.

Lydia smiled, and nodded.

"If the rapist returned and you had to decide whether to kill or to wound him, which would you do," Creighton asked.

"I would kill him," Lydia said, without hesitation.

"Why?" Creighton asked.

"Because I'm a mother and he threatened my children. He deserved justice and I would feel fine later," Lydia said.

"There is the justice of lawyers and the courtroom, and the justice of The Prophets and of God," Creighton said.

"Precisely," Lydia said.

I had been holding Creighton's arm and, when he spoke, I instinctively tightened my grip. He turned toward me.

"*What*?" he asked.

"I absolutely agree!" I said.

But it was more than that. His phrase was uttered during the TV interview of a retired Texas Ranger several months before. This sentiment caused Vladimir to insist that

I hire him. The program was widely broadcast and Creighton must have seen it.

Losing the parents with whom he had grown up had erased his past. This would confuse anyone since our past is who we are. Creighton was creating a new identity and I was pleased that his outlook on life mirrored that of Vladimir and me. I believed, beyond any doubt, that Vladimir was his biological father.

Chapter 155

Creighton's mental trauma had been severe. Discovering that his parents weren't who they said and then suddenly losing them had turned his world upside down. He had to struggle with all shades of gray. What is reality? Who is wrong and who is right? Who really loves me? Even whether he could decide who is telling the truth.

Creighton's memories of his past, which determine who one is, had been erased and he was furious. Some of his rage was, rightly, toward the parents that he grew up with. But some of his anger was directed at me and his real parents: If they had *really* loved me, why didn't they look harder to find me? he asked himself.

I didn't figure this out on my own. My meetings with Doctor Kandey helped. My fear of Creighton hearing details of Lydia's assault was reasonable since, psychologically, he had been raped too. I wanted to protect him. He is the only brother that I will ever have.

Thankfully, my fear wasn't justified for Creighton proved stronger than I expected. Lydia's words didn't re-traumatize him.

This caused me to change another decision. We (me, our mother, and Doctor Crowe) had believed that it would be best to shield Creighton from meeting too many strangers too soon. Now we gave in to his persistent demand to meet my adoptive family.

They hungered for this too. My parents wanted the son that they had longed for and my sisters wanted a brother.

Margaret in Manhattan

Doctor Crowe suggested that we reduce the stress of this meeting on Creighton. Since he would be the object of curiosity, it would be best to have many people present as during an ordinary social gathering. Erika's offer to host a party at her home was accepted and she instantly turned on her organizing manner. This had been her skill since high school.

In addition to my family, we invited Kimberly and Missy Rheese, my two best friends from Barnard. Both had young children though only Missy Rheese was married. Her husband and their kids were invited too.

I hadn't spoken with either of them in months. Missy Rheese, because she lived in Manhattan, and Kimberly, because she had been busy working at a local startup. Like Randy and Creighton, she is a computer nerd.

Though Kimberly is a great person, I wasn't sure that having her meet Creighton was a good idea. She is *too* beautiful and I had witnessed her seductive behavior with attractive men.

"*Oh, come on*, they could make *gorgeous* kids together," Erika had teased.

Chapter 156

It was another of Erika's elaborate parties. The basement had been turned into a fairy land containing snacks from Greenwich's foremost St. Moritz Bakery: Mini Red Velvet, Chocolate, and Vanilla cupcakes for the adults; and Owls, Pandas, and Pupcakes for the children. These animal image cupcakes are a big hit with kids.

Always practical, Erika had learned the children's sizes and provided them with gifts from around the world. Gucci kids' dresses, Stella McCartney Kids' sunglasses, and Salvatore Ferragamo Kids' shoes were among the presents. Like they say about the price of a yacht: If you need ask, you can't afford it.

While the kids snacked, the adults awaited Creighton's entrance. We had deliberately arrived late to spare him the stress of repeated introductions.

While driving, I described Erika's home lest he be frightened by the shotgun wielding guards.

"Erika's mother and sister were murdered when she was a child. Her father is obsessive about security and armed guards roam their home. You won't notice them after a while," I said.

"No problem," Creighton said.

I felt that I should add something.

"I've stayed over many times and experienced a few false alarms when it was feared that an intruder had gained entrance. If this happens, just follow instructions and you'll be safe. Vladimir's company manages the security and most of the guards are former military," I said.

I felt Creighton's stare before he spoke.

"Nothing could be worse than what happened in my life," he said, softly.

Creighton looked edgy as we approached the basement staircase.

"Don't worry. They'll all love you," I said, reassuringly.

He smiled hesitantly as all conversation ceased when we entered the room.

Chapter 157

One's life can change in an instant and that's what happened when Creighton saw Kimberly. Women stare at her designer clothes and men want to tear them off. Men would have fought duels for her in past centuries. Creighton stood frozen and stared.

Not that she wore something special that day. Just the timeless, sexy look of a white t-shirt, Chloé skirt, and gleaming gold leather net sandals. Her beauty and freshness of youth turned these casual (but expensive) clothes into high fashion.

Gripping his arm, I propelled us forward for the introduction that I feared since I knew what would happen. Creighton would fall for Kimberly, and fall hard.

Despite this worry, another thought entered my mind. Might that not be good for both since they are so similar? Both are brilliant, shy, and unusually attractive. And, as Erika had teased, they might make beautiful children together.

Moreover, considering Kimberly's vast wealth, if their relationship didn't work out, he wouldn't be caught on any financial hook. These thoughts enabled my smile as we stood before her.

"Kimberly, this is my brother, Creighton. He's hungered to meet you since you're a hacker too," I said.

I placed his hand on hers though fearing that she would move it onto her breast. Kimberly's social gawkiness doesn't extend to sex. But this didn't happen. She led him to a corner where they began speaking animatedly.

I permitted this for a minute. Then, despite his resistance, I pulled him away to meet the other guests.

Margaret in Manhattan

Creighton's instinctive courtesy and shyness won over everyone. My mother insisted that he spend a weekend at our home. My baby sister, Claudine, said that he could have her room, which is an important signal of liking from a child. From their frank, open-mouthed stares, I concluded that my older sisters wanted Creighton to share their bed.

Chapter 158

Few had been invited to the party. Just those whom Creighton would regularly see if he settled in Greenwich. This wasn't certain nor was my future location. If I returned to Barnard College the following term, Creighton might choose to live with me in Manhattan. The money that I had gained in Berlin enabled freedom for me and for those that I loved.

But Creighton might also choose to live with my adoptive family in Greenwich, becoming the son that they had longed for, and to experience a traditional family life. Or he might settle with Vladimir in Berlin, or with Peter in London.

Only Kimberly seemed settled. After being released from jail, she and her child had moved into Erika's home until buying one of her own which hadn't yet happened.

Though a busy, involved mother, her restless mind needed the stimulation of creative labor. She gained this by working at the local startup that Erika's father ("Hamilton, call me Harry") had invested in.

Harry savored company since the murder of his wife and older daughter years earlier. Kimberly and her child were welcome to remain at his home for as long as she wanted.

It was a comfortable arrangement for Kimberly too. The house was secure, which is a crucial consideration for the super-wealthy, and had the convenience of maid service and an ever-obliging cook. There were also close-by playmates for her daughter. What more could she want?

Well, maybe Creighton too, I thought, as they stood close. As Kimberly touched his arm and stared up into his eyes, Erika edged beside me.

"Kimberly would be good for him. She's more experienced and is less afraid of the world. They would be like you and Randy. Don't interfere," Erika whispered.

I nodded agreement. I didn't plan to. Still, before leaving, I whispered to Kimberly.

"Please don't hurt him," I said.

Chapter 159

Creighton was more excited and alive when the party ended. It was as if he had been a male Cinderella until Kimberly touched and awoke him.

Thankfully, she sensed Creighton's fragility and didn't push their relationship. I returned him to the hospital that evening, to serve his final days as a patient.

Like baby birds who have learned to fly, Creighton hungered to spread his wings. So, contrary to the initial plan, he spent the week before our flight at my adoptive parents' home. And everything went fine!

He took my room while I slept in Melody's. This gave us the chance to have our first real talk since I returned from Berlin.

Melody was having an identity crisis. A long-term movie lover, she had first wanted a job as a film critic and then any job in the movie industry. Realizing that just a pretty face wouldn't gain it, she decided to become an entertainment lawyer and, eventually, an "agent to the stars."

To this end, and with our lawyer-father's advice, she began working as a paralegal in a local law firm and found it excruciatingly boring. Our dad sought to reassure her, stating that most beginner jobs were tedious. She listened, and began self-medicating herself with marijuana while deciding on another career.

We spoke late that night, me lying in bed and her in the sleeping bag. That she had surrendered her bed indicated how desperately she needed our talk.

"I spoke with an Air Force recruiter yesterday," she said, suddenly.

"For a date, I'd understand, but you'd be crazy to sign up," I said.

"Why?"

"You couldn't stand the boredom of training and are too independent to take orders comfortably. Don't sign up! If you must sign somewhere, I'll drive you to Lena's mental hospital," I said.

It was a cruel statement but I wanted to be sure to get through to her. A military commitment isn't easily ended.

Melody was silent for a minute. She removed a joint from a small silver case, looked at me, and returned it. *That*, even our liberal father wouldn't accept at home.

"I can't stand my life. I must do *something*," Melody pleaded.

While staring down at her, an idea suddenly occurred to me.

"OK, quit your job and come with us to Europe," I said.

Chapter 160

Melody immediately perked up from surprise at my idea.

"*What?*" she asked.

"Creighton and I are leaving for Europe next week. We're stopping at London before going to Berlin. Come with us. The trip will clear your head and who knows what else? Where nothing awaits you, anything can happen," I replied.

Though adopting a confident tone, I felt uneasy speaking this way. Melody was older and I had relied on her advice in the past.

"I can't afford it," she said, with a wan smile.

"It's on me. I made some money in Berlin and what good is money if you can't spend it on those you love," I said.

"Travel is expensive. I won't use all your savings," Melody said.

"Let me worry about that. You just check about your passport and clothes," I said.

"I'll pay you back."

"No, you won't. It's my gift for all that you've done for me," I said.

"*Alright,*" she said, drawing out each syllable and smiling.

I turned out the light before she could ask the obvious questions: How much money do you have? How did you get it?

Margaret in Manhattan

She was a lawyer's daughter and shouldn't know. Though my twenty-one million dollars had been stolen from a wanted criminal, no legal system would have approved my actions. With less luck, I could have wound up in a German prison, side-by-side with Randy who had helped me.

Over the following days, my parents and sisters showed Creighton what family life was. He gorged on my mother's most elaborate meals and heard my father's greatest legal war stories. My sisters vied for his attention. It was, in Creighton's words, "the best time of my life."

Our flight for London left early and I had spent the prior morning with my biological mother, Lena.

"When will you have the test result?" I asked.

"Before you return, in two weeks," Lena replied.

"Call me the minute that you hear!" I insisted, though knowing that she wouldn't.

Bad news is best delivered in person.

Chapter 161

Nothing so raises the spirits as spending money and that's what I did. For our flight, I chose Lufthansa Airlines since their First-Class flights had the highest online ratings.

Our flight from Newark Airport left at 8:35AM. Erika insisted on driving us there though bitching about having to get up so early. She's the best.

"That's what friends are for," she had said.

The flight's expense was worth it. The First-Class cabin's eight seats were spread between two rows arranged in a 1-2-1 configuration. One seat was empty and the three of us occupied an entire row.

The other four seats were filled by a government official, a financier, and their assistants. Their professions were easily identified by their phone conversations before takeoff.

Creighton was nervous and excited since this was his first flight. Each seat had the trademark Lufthansa rose and a seventeen-inch video display. Soon after takeoff, a flight attendant set up a small bar at the front of the cabin though it wasn't self-serve.

Both the government official and the financier chose Johnnie Walker Blue Label whiskey. Later, Erika told me that it cost two-hundred-dollars a bottle on the ground. She learned such things from arranging her father's business parties.

Being Mormon and underage, I didn't drink. Melody did though she's Mormon too but I said nothing. I'm not her mother. Creighton also didn't drink. He was both underage and had leftover psychiatric medication in his system. We snacked on juice and crackers spread with caviar.

The touchdown was smooth but my worrying returned as soon as the plane landed. Although Peter had earlier learned of the parentage issue, I couldn't be sure how he would react. Nor could I predict his mother's response since she is of an older generation. Some of today's relationships were rare in her day.

Stop worrying for you'll soon find out, I told myself, as we entered the terminal.

Chapter 162

A sign reading, "Margaret and Creighton," was held by Mr. Jenkins who I immediately recognized from my last visit.

"Your grandmother is waiting with Peter in the car. Her ankle troubles her and she can't stand for long. Peter wouldn't leave her though no police officer would dare give her a ticket," he said, with a smile.

This was likely true. As a teenager, Victoria had been presented at Buckingham Palace and Peter is a national hero. Great Britain remains class conscious.

Mr. Jenkins is a retired Chief Inspector of the Metropolitan Police Force that covers London. He had earlier been a Scotland Yard detective. Now, he works only for my grandmother: investigating a prospective financial advisor or employee; driving her car; and serving as her bodyguard.

Both Peter and my grandmother address him as "Jenkins." Being American, I've never felt comfortable with this style or with his carrying my bags as a porter would. Yet, though always speaking to and of him as "Mr. Jenkins," I deferred to local custom and let him carry it. I had packed little and it wasn't heavy. In his view, I was the granddaughter of his stately boss.

Their car is an old, scrupulously maintained, four-door Jaguar. Victoria and Peter sat within. After my brief introductions of Creighton and Melody, we drove home.

Home was a four-story, white stucco house an hour away. Though looking small-town American, it has an unexpected interior with the property being entered by walking up stairs. There is a lower ground floor, a raised ground floor, and three floors above.

On the lower ground floor is a kitchen/breakfast room of about twenty by twenty-five feet. It has three windows, a tiled floor, recessed halogen spotlights, and the usual kitchen appliances which here includes a TV.

The ground floor holds a wine vault, a cellar, a sauna and shower, a gym, and two bedrooms. On the raised ground floor is an entrance hall, a reception room, a dining room, and a study.

The first floor holds a larger reception room of about twenty by forty feet, and a library. Bedrooms of varying size and dressing rooms are on the second, third, and fourth floors. There are also two terraces.

Upon arriving, further introductions were made: to Ellie, who had been Peter's nursemaid and now served as his mother's housekeeper; and to the live-in cook/handyman couple, Abigail and Liam.

"Why don't you rest until Tea," Victoria suggested.

It was a welcome idea.

Chapter 163

I occupied the same bedroom as during my earlier summer in London. It had been designed with what was believed an American teenager would love. "Sophisticated and understated with a Manhattan loft feel," the decorator had said.

The room had an orange chandelier, purple furnishings, striped curtains with funky flashes of color, and vintage film posters on the walls. For comfortable studying, there was a desk before an exposed brick wall.

The room was as much "me" as if it had a bassinet and Disney decals. But its comfortable four-poster bed makes up for the room's décor, I thought once again, as I plopped down.

Whether we were biologically related or not, I had grown to love Peter and Victoria. And, as with any relatives or friends, they would want to learn about my life since our last meeting. Questions would be asked though with typical British reserve. Sometimes, with just silence and an inquiring look.

Vladimir would have told Peter *something* about my involvements in Berlin since they worked together. I didn't know how much of this Peter had shared with Victoria. Maybe nothing, feeling this was my decision. Exhibiting good breeding through tactful behavior is a maxim of my English family.

Libby, one of Erika's acquaintances, is a compulsive liar. She lies about the most unimportant matters. Libby said this began when she was dating a jealous control freak. He was suspicious of whatever she did without him. He would scream if she told him that she was drinking wine at a girlfriend's apartment with another guy around.

So, gradually, she began leaving out details. First, that there had been a man in the room and later even the wine. There was no harm done, right? Except that Libby soon began lying even when she dated normal guys. Like *forgetting* that there was a guy present when she worked late in the office. Having one psycho boyfriend had turned her into a lying freak.

"You must *believe* in the lie for it to be believable," Libby advised Erika, who had told me.

Later, after arising from a two-hour nap, I tried to follow this advice during Tea.

Chapter 164

My grandmother, Victoria, is *very* proper so I took pains when dressing for Tea. Erika's going-away present had been a Career-Dressing Kit intended for a professional's workday. From it I selected the Lagarde 2.0 Shirt, the Foster Pants, and the Woolf Jardigan. Victoria would excuse jeans and t-shirt on Melody and Creighton. She hadn't educated them as she had me.

Before going downstairs, I practiced my lines: after study in Berlin, my mother had informed me that I have a twin brother and we spent recent weeks having fun.

This would be supported by the Valley Girl innocence that had become my second nature. Peter, who knew the facts, wouldn't buy this story but his mother might.

In the dining room, the table was set for Tea to which I had become accustomed. Tea is a hallowed ritual in England. Its centerpiece is a tiered cake stand on a floral tablecloth. There are floral Chinaware, lace dollies, and folded napkins. Before each chair, on a small plate, was a coconut and cinnamon place-name cookie iced with the guest's name.

Sugar and milk were on the table along with a variety of tea: English Breakfast, Earl Grey, herbal, fruit, chamomile, and peppermint.

For snacking, there were scones with jam (rhubarb and ginger, strawberry, cinnamon-scented plum) and clotted cream. For those with a bigger appetite, there were sandwiches on rye bread: carrot and raisin, and smoked salmon and avocado.

Margaret in Manhattan

The cake platform held tarts (apple-rose and raspberry), dark chocolate madeleines, lemon bars, cheesecake, and Seville meringue pie with pomegranate.

Everyone stood, having awaited my arrival, and I quickly apologized. Being late for meals is considered even more of a sin here than at home in Greenwich. But Victoria just smiled and all eyes turned to Creighton. I immediately feared what he might have revealed.

Chapter 165

I'm not one of those people who believe in weird events. Like the ones who insist that they've seen UFOs or a monster sea creature or frogs raining down. I used to place the belief that twins share a special bond within that category of strangeness. That twins thought similarly and could sense, even from a distance, when one of them was ill. But I no longer do.

Creighton had been the object of attention when I entered the dining room. Warmed by Victoria's hand on his arm and Peter's benevolent gaze, he shared an alleged story of his life. Even I, an acknowledged gifted liar, couldn't have done better.

Instead of being a sleeper-agent-in-training rescued from murderous parents, Creighton was the child of loving, hard-working, devout Christians. His mother had been a nurse and his father had been a truck driver.

While accompanying her husband on a cross-country delivery, both were killed when a drunken driver sideswiped their truck.

This happened when Creighton was fourteen. He then lived in a series of abusive foster homes until running away at sixteen. Thereafter, he supported himself by working as a software consultant, having taught himself programming since he was seven. Looking older and possessing critical skills, he had easily found free-lance jobs.

Creighton's story floored me and I couldn't resist commenting.

"How could you rent a place to live at your age?" I asked, feigning innocence.

"By doing what I had to do to survive though it bothered my conscience," Creighton said, adopting a contrite tone. "While living in a youth hostel, I stole the ID of an older boy who resembled me. But I never used it for anything illegal," he explained.

I arched my eyes and looked at Peter. Though knowing the real story, he merely winked and smiled. Whoever was his father, Creighton was truly my twin!

Chapter 166

As all attention focused on Creighton, I began feeling neglected and felt silly for this reaction. While visiting London last summer, *I* had been the center of interest. Now, Creighton was and Melody wasn't far behind. Both adored Peter and clung to his every word.

I understood Creighton's reaction since he hungered for the real father that he never had. But Melody's behavior puzzled me until I realized that she was relating to Peter as she did to every attractive man, even those who were unsuitable for dating.

Still, fortified by Victoria's summertime lessons on etiquette, I simply listened, smiled, and snacked.

When Tea ended, we went our separate ways. Melody latched onto Victoria and Creighton latched onto Peter. I went to my bedroom and called Erika.

"Mmm," was her response when she picked up the phone.

"Tell Clarence to get his mouth out of your groin," I said, in an irritated tone.

"Well, *you're* in a good mood," said Erika.

Erika and I are so close that neither feels the need to apologize for their occasional dopiness.

I remained silent until Erika asked, "What's wrong?"

"Everything it seems or maybe I'm just worn out. Too much has happened recently. Lena gets her medical test results any day, and there's more," I replied.

Silence followed until I spoke again.

"I'm getting moody and might be pregnant, this time for real. We haven't always been careful," I said.

"Have you tested yourself?" Erika asked.

"Not yet. I'll buy a kit but this time it'll have instructions in English," I said.

My last pregnancy test, a false positive, had been taken in Berlin.

"Have to go, dad's calling. We have a business dinner tonight. Let me know," Erika said.

I promised to do so, hung up, and lay down. I had been increasingly tired lately.

Chapter 167

Our visit in London went, as the English would say, "swimmingly." Victoria arranged a party to meet our relatives. Though all were near Peter's age since our few cousins were traveling abroad, it was still a pleasant day.

Creighton's fictitious life story engrossed everyone and he dodged uncomfortable questions with a skill that amazed me. Melody hung out in my bedroom the evening before we left for Berlin.

"I could easily love Creighton," she said.

"Incest is not necessarily best," I said.

"We're not related. How would it be incest?' she asked.

"OK, it wouldn't be incest. But sex would blow Creighton's mind. He looks great but is just hanging together," I replied.

"Others survive losing their parents. I would think that a girlfriend is just what he needed," Melody objected.

Melody had also believed Creighton's lies. The facts of his life had been shared on a need to know basis. She didn't need to know and I wouldn't tell her. So, not wanting to arouse her curiosity, I took the easy way out.

"Creighton loves Kimberly and she loves him. They've been an item since the moment they met," I said, solemnly.

Melody's face colored at my words.

"I'm sorry but it's important that you know. Being involved in a romantic triangle might blow his mind again," I said, regretfully.

Melody nodded acceptance. She was a big girl and knew the score. She changed the subject.

"I get depressed. You have someone. Erika has someone. Creighton has someone. Even Melanie, who is eight-years younger than me, has a boyfriend. What's wrong with me?" she asked.

Her tone was unselfish and I answered honestly.

"There's nothing wrong with you. You're beautiful and brilliant. It's just a matter of searching and luck," I said, meaning every word.

"Maybe I'll meet *him* in Berlin? If I keep moving with a lucky charm up my ass?" Melody asked, with a smile

"I'll be your wingman and do my best," I promised, also smiling.

I reached over and touched her hand. The sign of one woman to another saying, *we've got this*. I was being honest too: being Melody's matchmaker will keep my mind off my Lena, I thought.

Chapter 168

I felt at home at Berlin's Tegel Airport. This, even though it's small, outdated, deteriorated, and has a jammed parking lot. There are few shops and seats with nothing to do nearby. It's hard to believe that you are in the capital of Germany.

A terror bombing had occurred in Antwerp just days before and there was an atmosphere of potential attack. Polizei patrols carrying long automatic rifles, accompanied by K9 dogs, patrolled the area.

Still, Tegel is not all bad. It's closer to the center of Berlin than the alternate airport in Schoenefeld and the signage is clear. It's easy to get around and the tourist desk people are friendly.

Because of the security scare, our flight was delayed and we didn't arrive until after 11:00PM. Despite the lateness, Vladimir, his wife, Ulrika, and their young daughter who everyone calls Beauty, were on hand to meet us. Quick introductions were made before driving home.

Breakfast is served at 8;00AM, the cook informed us, with Teutonic efficiency. I looked at Ulrika, having planned to sleep until noon.

"You're here to enjoy yourselves! Come then as you are or whenever. You know where the kitchen is," she said, smiling.

I simply nodded, feeling too tired to respond, but it wouldn't have mattered. Here, as in London, Creighton was the center of attention. Beauty had sat beside him in the car, feigning fear and gripping his hand. Melody looked at me, having apparently the same thought: Beauty will be a knockout as a teenager!

Creighton's smile at Beauty had been a mixture of innocence and understanding. How much of my protecting does he really need? I asked myself.

Chapter 169

Early the next morning, I learned that Vladimir had his own opinion about Creighton's health. Though being worn-out, I had slept poorly, having been awakened by dreams that I couldn't remember. Finally, giving up, I went to the kitchen for a snack. Lately, I had been increasingly hungry for the unhealthy snacks that I usually ignored.

While passing the dining room, I peeked in and saw Vladimir. He was drinking coffee and reading his daily newspaper, *Die Welt*. In the kitchen, I poured myself a glass of orange juice and then went and sat opposite him. He looked up and put down his paper.

"Creighton isn't in good shape," he said, slowly.

This seemed both statement and question.

"No, though he looks OK. Whatever their faults, my adoptive parents did a good job. I know who I am and aren't afraid of the world. Creighton doesn't and is.

"He's smart but is an emotional wreck like my friend, Kimberly, used to be. She's fallen for him and it might be good for both of them so long as she goes slow. He couldn't handle a heavy romance now," I said.

"Would martial arts training reduce his fears?"

"Maybe, if he's interested. But he's mostly an intellectual like Randy," I replied.

"His fears may not be of the world but of what's going on inside him. His parents behaved destructively even before their intention to murder him. He must still be furious and afraid that his rage would boil over, maybe even toward a lover. He might fear that he would be a danger to women and they would be a danger to him. It's a challenge," Vladimir said.

"That was pretty much his doctor's opinion too," I said, with surprise.

"Don't be shocked. Not all generals are idiots," Vladimir said, with a small smile.

Chapter 170

Ulrika had intended to host a welcoming party for Creighton, with a hundred guests at a local hotel. But after hearing Vladimir's concern about Creighton's fragility, she made a smaller affair. A few relatives along with some of Vladimir's business associates and their families were invited. Having children present would keep the atmosphere informal and playful, she thought.

The party was on Saturday. To give us a restful night, we checked into the Pullman Hotel Berlin on Friday. Though the hotel is a bit old, our rooms were large, the beds were comfortable, the staff was friendly, the food was great, the shower was the best that I ever had, and the pool and spa were amazing.

The hotel is close to the zoo and aquarium, in the Tiergarten part of Berlin. It was five stars all the way, in my opinion.

To reduce Creighton's time "onstage," the party was scheduled for only three hours beginning at 3PM. With her usual thoughtfulness, Ulrika had rented a suite where the youngest children could nap. Babysitters and security guards were present for their parents' comfort.

Here, there was no receiving line like at Victoria's party. Instead, Creighton and Melody were introduced informally.

Huge, imposing Borya "adopted" Creighton almost immediately and resisted leaving his side. Borya's only son, a young military pilot, had been killed in Syria the previous year.

Margaret in Manhattan

I moved close, thinking to draw Creighton away from Borya if he seemed uncomfortable. But my attention wasn't needed. Their conversation concerned the Russian foods: Borscht (beet and cabbage red soup), and Shuba (salted herring covered with layers of grated boiled vegetables, beets, onions, and mayonnaise).

These dishes were new to Creighton. Borya delighted in introducing him to them, as a parent would to a young child, and Creighton glowed in the attention. Ulrika sidled over and drew me aside.

"It looks like Creighton has gained another father," she murmured.

"One can't have too many good fathers," I said, nodding agreement.

Chapter 171

We lazed in Berlin for a week. During that time, Vladimir and Borya dragged Creighton to small parties. But these were all business and lacked the social demands of meeting family.

"Many computer people were there. I had fun," Creighton excitedly told me.

"They want to hire you," I said.

"I understood that but they don't have a chance. Berlin and Moscow don't appeal to me like Greenwich right now," he said.

Whether this feeling arose from wanting to be close to me or to his mother or to Kimberly didn't matter to me.

The staggering news came from Melody. She had, in her words, "met the love of my life," and without any help from me. But it wasn't this that bothered me.

Josef had several drawbacks, as I viewed them. He was fourteen years older than Melody and had been married twice. His three children lived with him and their mother's whereabouts was unclear.

His good points were that he was educated, having a Master's Degree from the London School of Economics, and came from a wealthy, long-established family.

They had met at one of Borya's parties, Josef's company was doing business with the Russian government. Melody didn't know what this involved but, knowing Borya's usual activities, I could guess.

Margaret in Manhattan

In the past, it had never worked when I tried to warn girls away from their unsuitable boyfriend. I just wound up losing a friend. Few things can so blind women as the glow from a handsome, interested man and men who are believably sincere are halfway there. Josef was skillful in love-making too.

Thus I simply listened while Melody babbled on about his charms, hoping that an opportune time to interfere would present itself. Finally, feeling frustrated, I raised the problem with Ulrika.

"Melody has gone crazy! What can I do?" I asked, after describing my concern.

Ulrika gave me her most charming smile. Before becoming pregnant with Vladimir's child, she had been his most skillful agent.

"You go to war," she said, sweetly.

Chapter 172

Ulrika can be a *serious* enemy. You don't ever want to get her pissed at you. Her plan was simple. Sensing that Josef was a player, she provided enough evidence to convince even love-struck Melody of this.

Using her contacts, Ulrika hired a gorgeous hooker to seduce Josef. Ulrika then, anonymously, sent a video of their activities to Melody with the expected result.

Ulrika then gave us a mother-daughter lecture unlike any that we had experienced. It lightened Melody's mood and she managed a smile.

"Finding a good lasting love is a matter of luck and timing. Three kinds of women have a problem doing this and neither of you fit into these categories.

"Some women seem always to date messed-up guys. Those with long-hair who are forever stoned, the kind of guy who'll fart to show they're happy to see you. These women eat peanut butter for dinner and drink too much. Basically, they can't live alone and need someone to take care of them.

"Then there are the women who meet perfect guys but always manage to find something wrong with them. They're too fussy. They'll reject him even if he's smart and funny and has a great job and teeth and fucks like the horniest eighteen-year-old on their first girl.

"But, she decides, they have a characteristic that she *can't stand*. Maybe it's that his first serious date was named Eileen, or that he constantly updates his Facebook status, or that he said something she hated like 'I want to spend all day with my head on your tummy.' There is just something *awful* about him.

"Finally, there's the nasty woman who has been alone too long because she has impossible tastes. Like wanting a millionaire who is no more than two years older and had little experience with women and so will adore her. These women won't settle for anyone less.

"But you girls don't fit into any of these categories so stop worrying and get off your butts and let's go shopping."

And that's what we did.

Chapter 173

KaDeW*e* (Kaufhaus des Westens, or Department Store of the West) is the second largest department store in Europe. It is in the district of Schöneberg in northwest Berlin, where Albert Einstein lived for twenty years.

KaDeWe has eight floors. Two are devoted entirely to food and we went there first. Beauty was cranky and Ulrika suggested that we eat before shopping. We had barely sat down when Erika phoned.

"Margaret?"

Even with the noisy room and static-filled connection I could note the panic in her voice.

"Yes. Erika? What's wrong?"

"She's dead...hour ago...body..."

My heart lost a beat. My mother, Lena, had died. *Medical test, cancer, I'll never see her again*. The thoughts jumbled through my mind.

When the connection was suddenly broken, I frantically dialed Lena's number even as I realized how illogical this was since she was dead. But she answered her phone on the second ring.

"*Momma*?" I screamed.

"Margaret, what's wrong?"

"Erika just phoned on a bad connection. I thought she said you'd died. What did the clonality test show?"

A positive test result meant that Lena's original diagnosis of the deadly cancer, SPTCL (subcutaneous panniculitis-like T-cell lymphoma) was correct.

"I have panniculitis, not cancer. It's a trivial inflammation of the fat cells and no treatment is needed," Lena said, and I heard relief in her voice.

"Lena is OK. The test results show that she doesn't have cancer," I told the others, who had been silently staring at me.

"Erika probably spoke of Catherine's death," Lena said.

"*Who*?" I asked, quickly, before remembering.

Catherine was the mother of another of my best friends, Hillary. I couldn't understand. Catherine had been healthy when I last saw her only two months before!

There were several moments of silence before Lena spoke again.

"Her body was just found. She had been raped and murdered."